THE EYE WITH WHICH THE UNIVERSE BEHOLDS ITSELF

THE SECOND BOOK OF THE APOLLO QUARTET

Ian Sales

Whippleshield Books
www.whippleshieldbooks.com
UK

Published by Whippleshield Books
www.whippleshieldbooks.com

ISBN 978-0-9571883-4-1 (limited)
ISBN 978-0-9931417-1-3 (paper)
ISBN 978-0-9571883-5-8 (ebook)

Edited by Jim Steel
Cover by Kay Sales (kaysales.wordpress.com)

Second edition: January 2015

VI.
I am the eye with which the Universe
Beholds itself, and knows it is divine;
All harmony of instrument or verse,
All prophecy, all medicine, is mine,
All light of art or nature; - to my song
Victory and praise in its own right belong.
from 'Hymn of Apollo', 1820
Percy Bysshe Shelley

ABBREVIATIONS

A7LB the spacesuit worn by Apollo astronauts
AFB Air Force Base
AGC Apollo Guidance Computer
APS Ascent Propulsion System
CDR Commander
CM Command Module
CMP Command Module Pilot
COAS Crewman Optical Alignment Sight
CSM Command/Service Module
CWG Constant Wear Garment
DAC Data Acquisition Camera
DPS Descent Propulsion System
DSKY Display and Keyboard for the AGC and LGC
EOI Earth Orbit Insertion
EVA Extra Vehicular Activity
FDAI Flight Director Attitude Indicator
IV Intra-vehicular
LCG Liquid Cooling Garment
LEO Low Earth Orbit
LGC Luna Guidance Computer
LOS Loss Of Signal
MCC Mission Control Centre
MEVA Mars Excursion Visor Assembly
MGC Mars Guidance Computer
MM Mars Module
MOI Mars Orbit Insertion
NSA National Security Agency
OWS Orbital Workshop
PLSS Personal Life Support System
PNGS Primary Navigation and Guidance Section
PPK Personal Preference Kit

POTUS President of the United States
RCS Reaction Control System
SPS Service Propulsion System
TOI Transfer Orbit Insertion
USAF United States Air Force
USN United States Navy
VHF Very High Frequency
VOX Voice Operated eXchange (switch)

1999 This time, when he returns home he knows she will have left him for good. Her decision weighs on him still, even as the J-2 engine ceases its muted roaring and the force pressing him into his seat abruptly vanishes. She has threatened to leave him before, many times; and she came so very close when he returned from Mars. Somehow they have stayed together. The fight four nights ago was the worst for a long time—she'd been in the right and he'd known it, which only made him argue all the more fiercely. After Mars, she had told him never again would she sit at home worried and afraid, putting on a brave face for the press, living a lie that consumed her, that consumed her from within like acid—

But he could not refuse this mission.

Someone bumps his elbow, and his attention returns to the here and now. His hands have lifted from the arms of his seat, and he can no longer feel the pull of the Earth. To his left, the mission commander, Carl J Springer, ex-USN, stares fixedly at the control panel from within the polycarbonate bowl of his helmet. In the right-hand seat, the systems engineer, Anna Gibson, has a gloved hand up to a switch beside a line of three thumb-wheels. He should know the function of the switch, but his training was rushed and it has been a long time since he last flew in space. It is only when Gibson says, Gimbals off, that he remembers the panel's purpose. He does not know this

Apollo spacecraft as well as he once did; but it's not like it really matters—

Brigadier General Bradley Emerson Elliott, USAF, is the most senior officer aboard this spacecraft but he occupies the centre seat because he has the least senior role in its crew. He is the navigator.

Elliott is also a passenger on this flight. And he is going on a journey much further than his two crewmates.

Much, much further.

But, like his crewmates, he has tasks to perform. Springer and Gibson have already begun the Post-Orbit Insertion Checks on page 2-11 of the Launch Checklist—first the SPS Gimbal Motors, then a line of six switches for the abort system and emergency detection system from AUTO to OFF, disabling the various pyros on the spacecraft, making safe the systems they will not need for the rest of the flight. Elliott must do his bit, so he punches Verb 06 Noun 62 into the guidance computer DSKY to perform the first of these:

H_A 100.8, H_p 96.4, RV_I 25490, he tells Mission Control.

Capcom acknowledges his figures.

We got pitch up to horizontal, says Springer.

APS firing for orb rate, adds Gibson.

Houston, we are configured for orbit, Springer confirms.

The three of them work their way through the Launch Checklist, step by step, reconfiguring the spacecraft from its launch settings, readying it for its stay in orbit.

Once they have finished their tasks, Springer says, still gazing up at the control panel: Anna, you want to take your helmet and gloves off?

Cabin pressure looks good, replies Gibson; Sure.

There is a moment of silence. Gibson then adds, You the one got the helmet stowage bags, Carl.

Now that it is permitted, Elliott unlocks and removes his gloves, then reaches up to his helmet locking ring. He lifts the helmet from his head, and is briefly fazed by its lack of weight. He holds his breath a moment, and then breathes in cautiously through his nose. The cabin air is cold and stings his sinuses. He smells hot metal and plastic, the odour of electronics hard at work, some oil, cleaning fluids, and the rubber and sweat stink rising from the neck of his spacesuit.

He sits, strapped into his seat, his arms thickly padded in the many layers of the A7LB and pressing against those of his neighbours, and watches his upturned helmet float in the air before him. He looks away from its transparent curves, his eyes refocus... and the momentary fuzziness prompts a claustrophobia which seems to shrink his spacesuit until it presses uncomfortably upon every square inch of his body. He is hemmed in, confined, *imprisoned*. His world too is close, too close, and defined solely by what he sees: grey and grey panels, filled with switches and dials and readouts, and the great white presences of his two crewmates to either side. Over there, a small window lit with the nacreous blue of the Earth below, a blueness perverse in its unearthliness, is further proof, if the freefall isn't enough, that this is no simulation.

Elliott wants to feel excitement at being in space again, the sense of adventure he felt the first time he made orbit back in the 1970s. He wants that adrenalin high, the one that grips his heart in a vice, sharpens his vision to a knife-edge, and drains him of all emotion; and he wants to feel calm, collected, brimful of the "Right Stuff", professional, laconic, a goddamn *astronaut.*

He needs to feel many things, but the journey he is about to take fills him with numb dread. Such a distance, beyond imagining. And *he* once travelled one hundred and fifty million miles to Mars, and more back. At the time, that number seemed beyond comprehension.

But: fifteen light-years.

88,120,000,000,000 miles.

Approximately.

He can barely say it: *eighty-eight trillion miles.*

He sits, strapped into his seat, as the Apollo CSM and its S-IVB fly about the Earth, one orbit every ninety-five minutes, and he knows that soon the J-2 will relight and put them on their transfer orbit to L5 and the space station located there. And he's reminded of those final orbits before his Mars Orbit Insertion burn twenty years ago, in a spacecraft of a much earlier generation than this one—

As the CSM speeds about the Earth, Elliott wants to rubberneck and see the world below him in all its life-sustaining diversity and colour, but Springer and Gibson are busy readying the spacecraft for TOI as if they've seen the view many times before. So for three hours, Elliott remains strapped into his seat, doing his bit, and trying to maintain a professional demeanour, a gravitas in freefall, appropriate to his age and rank, until, right on schedule at MET 003:21:09, the S-IVB's J-2 relights for Transfer Orbit Insertion.

Three days of coasting at 34,223 feet per second now await them. Springer gives permission for shirtsleeves. They unstrap from their seats, and float about the narrow spaces of the Command Module, slotted between seats and control panel or seats and Lower Equipment Bay. Gibson is first to remove her spacesuit, and Elliott abruptly discovers he does not know what to do. He can't treat her like "one of the guys" and has to look away as she wriggles out of her A7LB in the LEB, strips off her LCG and pulls on her cotton constant wear coveralls.

Once she is done, it is Elliott's turn. He looks up halfway through pushing his spacesuit's legs down his hips to see Gibson grinning at him, and he reaches out a hand and spins himself about so his back is to her before he finishes undressing.

Elliott gazes out of a horizon window as behind him Springer gets into his constant wear garment and Gibson makes low-voiced jokes about privacy. There is nothing to see outside; there is everything to see outside. The universe—*creation*—across which is spilled a thick splash of stars, and he thinks about unimaginable distances and the deadly vacuum of space inches from his face.

There is nowhere else he would rather be.

He has missed this—the freedom of freefall, the sense of purpose that comes from following mission checklists, the constant marvel of human engineering, the desperate desire to find a place for humanity in an implacable and indifferent universe.

Gibson's low female murmur puts him in mind of Judy, and he wishes his wife could be with him here and now, but he can't picture her—Judy always so neat and well-dressed, Judy always so carefully made-up—he can't imagine her in Gibson's place, Gibson with her boyish features fresh as air, her earthy swagger, her dark hair a mermaid's corona. And as Elliott thinks of his wife, he regrets she refuses to understand why he had to accept this mission, he is hurt she feels the only response available to her is to walk out on him; and he wishes he could feel some connection stretching from here to the home he shares—shared—with Judy... But whatever hold their house at Edwards AFB, their life together, has on him it's growing thinner and more strained with each mile he travels from the planet.

It's a kind of freedom, he thinks; a freedom from earthly concerns as distance lessens his past life's hold on him, though he will never ignore or forget her—and it occurs to him NASA named its space station well. Fourteen years it has floated alone at a Lagrangian Point, space flotsam occupying one of the Solar System's tideless nodes. Elliott has read about Space Station Freedom, the only permanent US presence in space, but only in science magazines and colour supplements. He has been out of the loop since he left the Astronaut Corps back in 1982 and, until he'd begun training for this mission, he had not missed it.

Space Station Freedom is not visible, of course; it is still hundreds of thousands of miles away, as far from the Earth as the Moon. He cannot see the Moon either—and he has never seen it from any closer than LEO. He wonders what might have happened had he one day walked on its regolith. Would he have ever set foot on the surface of

Mars?

Would he be here now, just shy of sixty years old, about to go on the longest journey of his life?

1979 One hundred days after departing Earth orbit, thirty days before they reach Mars, Major Bradley Emerson Elliott, USAF, says farewell to his crewmate, Commander Robert Franklin Walker, USN. They shake hands, good solid bone-crushing grips, but superstitiously make no mention of luck or fortune. They possess total faith—in their own abilities, in the hardware, in the pencil-necks back on Earth. Neither doubts for an instant they will do this thing, both confidently anticipate a splashdown after a successful mission.

Elliott takes one last look around the hab module, his home for the past three months: its gridwork decking, its lockers and cubicles, its dumb up/down orientation as if designed for use in a gravity field; and then swims through the docking tunnel on the forward bulkhead and into the Mars Module. He's wearing his spacesuit, but without helmet and gloves. He'll put them on for the undocking, but for now he needs the dexterity of ungloved hands to perform the last few checks and programming changes to the MM. They've simulated the undocking twice before—on the day they pressurised and powered up the MM for the first time a week ago, and two days previously when they performed a full systems check of the spacecraft.

As he dives toward the floor of the MM, Elliott hears Walker close the tunnel hatch behind him. He somersaults clumsily until he is oriented as if about to fly the spacecraft. He pushes himself down until the soles of his boots touch the velcro on the floor and he sticks, but it doesn't feel secure. He stands at the commander's position and peers through the window before him. There is nothing to see: Ares 9 is hurtling towards Mars but the Red Planet is ahead of them, beneath his feet in fact, and so out of sight.

The earphones in Elliott's communications cap crackle—

Can you read me, Discovery?

Got you, Endeavour. Loud and clear.

We got a minute to go, Brad. You want to verify your hatch closed?

Wait, let me get the umbilicals... Right, closed and locked.

Okay, I'll vent the tunnel.

Give me a 06 20?

Sure... here's the angles: 35955, 10752, 36102. Got that? Um, MET is 2405:08:59. Brad, can you confirm tunnel is vented?

Let me get them down—uh, 35955, 10752, 36102. That right? And yeah, tunnel is vented, Bob.

Yep, you got 'em.

Okay, I got P47 up. I'm ready.

Ten seconds.

Roger. Going for soft undock.

Looking good.

Releasing capture latches...

What's your 06 83 say?

Nice and neat Sep.

[laughter] Just the way I like it.

That's it, I'm on my own now, Bob. See you in about two months. Starting Mars Intersection Sequence Intialisation...

There is something unreal about all this, preparing a spacecraft to land on Mars while still in interplanetary space, still thirty-five million miles from the destination. Once all the final changes have been made to the Mars Guidance Computer and the MM's PNGS, Elliott will put on his gloves and helmet, check the integrity of his spacesuit... and then he's go for hard undock. The MM, such an ungainly spacecraft, waiting impatiently in the saucer of the heatshield; it will separate from the flyby spacecraft, and Elliott will use the RCS to put the MM on an intercept course with Mars.

For now, his head is full of figures as he patiently punches VERB number NOUN number into the DSKY. He has the checklist in front of him, and he works his way through it methodically, as he has done numerous times before in simulation. And as he looks up at the control panel, and the "8-ball" FDAI centred in it, he remembers he has one task not on the checklist. Digging into the pocket on the right bicep of his spacesuit, he pulls out a folded photograph. He opens the photo and tries to press it flat on the Attitude Controller arm-rest with both hands, but all he does is rip free of the velcro and rise up toward's the MM's ceiling. Annoyed, he pushes his feet back down to the floor but his boots do not stick. He attaches the restraint cables to the D-rings at his waist, locks the ratchets, and now he is held down firmly and securely. But the photo has lifted from the arm-rest and is floating before the commander's window. He plucks it from the air, and tries again to flatten it, this time successfully. And he stands there, held in place by thirty pounds of force from the restraint cables, his thumbs and forefingers framing three sides of a creased and much-thumbed photograph. It's a picture of Judy, of course. He brought a dozen with him in his Personal Preference Kit, but this is his favourite. He has spent many hours staring at it over the past one hundred days, floating in his compartment, needing solitude, needing time away from Franklin. The photo shows her standing by the French windows of their house in Nassau Bay. The sun shines through the glass behind her, forming a golden halo about her long blond hair. She is smiling, but it is a weary smile. He can no longer remember what day he took the photo or for what reason—perhaps they were going somewhere, a neighbour's, a restaurant, he cannot recalls. Judy always dresses well, the smart dress and heels are no clue. He puts a finger to his wife's torso, and knows he will see her again. He is coming back, of that he is certain. She was angry when he was given command of Ares 9 and she stayed hurt right up to the moment he launched; but she will forgive him.

He slides a corner of the photo under an edge of one of the control panels. Judy will watch over him during the next thirty days as he flies towards Mars in this box with walls twice as thick as a soda can's. Apollo was dangerous—Apollo 13 proved that. But Lovell, Swigert and Haise got home, the pencil-necks brought them home. That was easy, that was local.

There is no hope of rescue on this mission.

1999 I see we got a regular hero visiting, says the man in the docking adaptor.

The nametag on his constant wear garment reads Parazynski. It is not a name Elliott knows, but then he has been out of the Astronaut Corps for nearly two decades.

Parazynski puts out a hand and grasps the hatch coaming just behind him. His other hand he raises in a salute. Welcome aboard, sir, he says; and this time his voice has the deference due to a person of Elliott's rank and achievements.

A second astronaut appears in the module through the hatch behind Parazynski, a woman. Her dark hair floats about her head like a sable nimbus.

We got us the first man on Mars here, Parazynski tells her, his gaze still on Elliott.

The *only* man on Mars, Elliott corrects. He is trying to

keep the tone light, but there is a bite to Parazynski's words and Elliott wonders what he has done to deserve it.

Yeah, damn shame we never went back, Parazynski replies.

Could it be envy? It has been many years since Elliott was a member of NASA and he does not know what narrative has been written internally about his missions, past and present. Ares 9 may have been a one-off, he wants to say; but Americans have visited other stars, there is even an inhabited base on an exoplanet orbiting one.

Elliott knows this because that is where he is going.

Parazynski spins about and pushes himself through the hatch, bringing himself to a halt by his fellow astronaut. She has one foot to the floor and one hand to the ceiling—according to Elliott's orientation, that is. Elliott can now see her name tag: it reads Weber. Another name unfamiliar to him.

Elliott follows Parazynski and Weber from the docking adaptor and into the module, a long cylinder walled, floored and roofed with lockers and screens and loops of wires. A tied bundle of cables and a slowly undulating fabric duct run along one corner and then dive down and through the hatch at the far end. Weber leads them into another docking adaptor, and as he joins her, Elliott looks up, sees an open hatch and, through it, what appears to be the interior of a Lunar Module. They are hundreds of thousand of miles from the Moon, and no one has been on the lunar surface for almost thirty years. He is about to ask, when Weber arrows down through a hatch in the floor, closely followed by Parazynski. Elliott pulls himself across to the hatch in the floor, then with a yank of both arms propels himself into the module below—

—and suffers a moment of vertigo as what was a vertical shaft full of clutter abruptly becomes a horizontal tunnel. Weber and Parazysnki have already disappeared through another hatch at the far end, and Elliott wonders how extensive this space station is. True, it has been in place

20

now for fifteen years, and has been added to on a regular basis...

He is surprised the space station does not smell; all those years and its interior looks tired and battered, with its snaking wires and hoses and far too many broken consoles, strips of duct tape and pieces of cardboard. But there is no odour at all, and he belatedly realises the air he is breathing is constantly on the move. Perhaps in some niche, where a pool of still air has gathered, some strange smell specific to freefall living might be found.

Through the hatch and this is the largest and untidiest module yet. The far end is sealed; it is the end of the line. There is a low table covered in velcro strips and double-sided duct-tape on the "floor" in amongst equipment Elliot cannot identify.

I guess, Parazynski says, you can tell us what brings you here.

Elliott reaches for something to halt himself, and puts a hand to a rail running along one wall. Once he is stationary, he says, The Robert H Goddard is taking me to Earth Two.

You must be a real important guy.

No, I have a real important job to do.

And they picked you because?

Elliott does not answer but looks about him and wonders why there is no window in this module. Do they not want to look out? He remembers a famous photograph of the Earth rising above the lunar horizon, taken by the crew of Apollo 8, Christmas 1968. A blue marble, so small and fragile, and the greatest distance from which the planet had ever been seen at that time. The Earth in that photo would be approximately the same size as the Earth seen from Space Station Freedom.

You're USAF, right? asks Parazynski.

Elliott nods, then watches as Weber consults a wristwatch and then porpoises about and launches herself at the open hatch. She swims from view.

Parazynski continues, You ever been to Area 51?

Again, Elliott nods, but cautiously. He has visited Groom Lake Air Force Base several times in his capacity as commander of the Air Force Flight Test Center at Edwards AFB. He has even seen some of the classified aircraft projects being developed and tested at Area 51.

Parazynski says, That's where the Serpos were invented, right?

A part of Area 51, yes, Elliott replies, called S4. But I don't have clearance for there.

Is it true, Parazynski asks, the Rocks use technology reverse-engineered from some flying saucer shot down in New Mexico in 1947?

Rocks? he asks.

The Goddard, the Webb and the Paine—the Rocks.

Elliott knows for a cold hard fact the secret Serpo engine which allows the "Rocks" to travel faster than the speed of light has nothing to do with any flying saucer, but he is not about to reveal it.

That's classified, he says.

He has heard of the crash at Roswell, New Mexico, and knows of the part it plays in UFO lore, but he's always believed it was a weather balloon. If USAF wants to use that myth to hide a bigger secret, the true origin of the Serpo engine... It's typical of the creative use of misinformation with which the US military protects its most closely-guarded secrets.

Someone appears in the hatch and, grateful for the interruption, Elliott turns to watch them enter the module. It is another member of the space station's crew. He is wearing a communications cap and his nametag reads Young. He is older than Parazynski and Weber, but still a decade or so short of Elliott's own fifty-eight years. The man's mouth is a tight line, his face expressionless.

You going on the Goddard? he asks.

Yeah, replies Elliott.

It's not due to depart for three weeks, Young says.

Elliott tells him, This is urgent. They should be prepping

now.

Young scowls. They don't tell us shit, he complains. I guess you can't either?

Elliott shrugs. Classified, he says. You know how it is.

Yeah, says Young. Fuck.

1980 After twenty days, Elliott smells a little ripe, as does the interior of his spacesuit. Three times now, he has undressed and given himself a sponge bath. And each time, it has taken an effort of will to struggle back into his A7LB. He would sooner wear a CWG, of course, and shower regularly, as he did aboard the flyby spacecraft. But the MM's cabin is only 235 cubic feet and he has to spend seventy days cooped up in it and all he has is a sponge, recycled water and a bar of soap. He has to wear his spacesuit constantly because the walls of the Mars Module are so thin a micrometeorite could easily pierce them. The five layers of his spacesuit also provide a better shield against radiation than the thin cotton of a Constant Wear Garment.

If not for the freefall, these past weeks—his first Christmas and New Year alone; and so far from another human being—would have been unbearable. He at least has the full volume of the cabin in which to move around. He misses Walker's presence, though it's been good to get some real solitude after one hundred days in the flyby spacecraft. They'd never have made it if they were just amiable strangers—no, they're best buds, a true team. All the same, he's not looking forward to the 537 days of the return journey...

The mission planners have given him plenty of science to occupy him, but his tools are necessarily limited and he's only done as tasked in a desperate attempt to stave off cabin fever. It hasn't really worked. Instead, he has spent hours staring out the commander's window at Mars, a rusty globe smeared with umber lines and shadows, growing larger and larger each day. He can see surface features now, Valles Marineris a cicatrix stitched across the planet's face, Mons Olympus so high its peak pokes out the atmosphere, the Tharsis Bulge... and the blurred swirls of a vast dust storm drifting across Chryse Planitia.

He and Walker talk every day, and together they check each system again and again and again. His course is programmed into the MGC, the numbers put together by much smarter guys back in Houston than the two of them. He trusts them, he has no choice, there is no way he can manually fly this spacecraft across millions of miles of space and hit his target. Periodically, he checks his IMU and feeds the figures to Walker, who passes them onto Houston. And sometimes they come back with updates he has to input on the DSKY. And every day, minute by minute, hour by hour, Mars draws closer, expands in the windows, its baleful presence gradually, inescapably, blotting out the heavens.

It's an astonishing act of faith, he belatedly realises, to imagine this mission will succeed, that he will spend nine days on the Martian surface, and then return safely to the Earth.

Yet his conviction is unshakeable. Nothing will go wrong because the engineering is up to the job. He's heard the stories, he knows how the space programme used to be run—Gus Grissom's "Do good work", and then the lemon and the Apollo 1 fire; even Alan Shepard's crack about "built by the lowest bidder"... But he knows how they built Ares 9, he was involved in the design, he visited the suppliers, he saw the parts being made, inspected them, ensured they met specification, and worked precisely as designed; and if he had not been confident in the hardware, Elliott would never have accepted the mission. Not even to be the first man on Mars.

Or so he told Judy.

The days pass and the photo of his wife on the control panel keeps him company as the Red Planet swells in the

24

windows until it fills his entire view. Once a week, he speaks to Judy, his S-Band signal relayed through the flyby spacecraft. She asks him how he is, he assures her he is fine, not mentioning he grows weaker with each day he spends in freefall and he worries he may not be strong enough to move about on the Martian surface. She tells him neighbourhood gossip, but he doesn't recognise the names, or recalls them only dimly, and their house in Nassau Bay seems like a distant memory and only Judy, kept fresh by the photograph, is clear in his memory—so much so she comes to represent home, Earth, the life he left behind and to which he is determined to return.

Now he's hurtling towards a curved plain of russets and ochres and reddish-browns, and soon he's so close all hint of curvature has gone. After one last report to Walker, he positions himself at the commander's station, attaches the waist restraints, and waits for the Mission Timer to hit 31234315, when the DSKY will tell him the MGC is running the descent program.

As the MM skims across the top of Mars' atmosphere, he has one hand to the thrust/translation controller and the other to the attitude controller, but he's not flying this craft. He looks down on the planet, and he's spent so long training for this he's used to the montages from the simulator, but now the landscape of Mars is written so emphatically across its face he can pick out major features and it all seems perversely unreal. The three Tharsis Montes: Arsia, Pavonis and Ascraeus; and now Noctis Labyrinthus, Hesperia Planum... It amuses him the Latin names sound so scientific, but translated into English they describe a fantasy land: Peacock Mountain, the Labyrinth of the Night, the Lands to the West...

The MM begins to vibrate and rattle as its heatshield hits wisps of Martian air. The atmosphere here is only fourteen miles deep and less than one percent as dense as Earth's. It's not enough to slow him from his interplanetary dash—but the designers have that covered. There's a rocket engine in the heatshield and it fires on schedule, dropping the MM through the Sound Barrier, and he's briefly amused at the thought of a sonic boom rolling unheard across the lifeless hills of Lunae Planum.

He watches the altimeter and rate of descent meter. It's a rough ride and his wasted muscles are making it hard to cope. The heatshield ablates as he hurtles across the Martian sky. He can see an orange glow from below, but is that the Martian surface or the heatshield burning? And now a white fireball envelopes the MM. This spacecraft was not designed for atmospheric entry, not even an atmosphere as thin as Mars'. It's two hundred and fifty times thinner than Earth, but it's still air, it's not a vaccum, and this flimsy thing was originally built to land on the airless Moon.

At least he's not experiencing the crushing Gs of an Earth re-entry. After thirty days in freefall with no exercise, it's a real strain, and his legs are aching, he's feeling a little light-headed, but he knows it feels much worse than it is so he rides it out—

Now the MM is in freefall, dropping towards the Martian surface. The spacecraft shudders as the heatshield is discarded. The MM is still flying descent stage first, so all he can see in the window is dark sky. A moment later, the spacecraft rocks as the drogue chutes are released. The MM jerks from side to side as the chutes open, there is a moment of vertiginous stability as the spacecraft falls for more than 15,000 feet, and then the drogue chutes are gone, work done, and he hears a loud bang as the mortars fire and the main chutes deploy.

The MM drops toward the surface with the chutes reefed for several long seconds, then the reef lines are cut and the chutes open to their full extent. The sudden deceleration is worse than he expected, his knees buckle and he has to lock them to avoid falling, and he swears as his forearm slides from the arm-rest and bangs against the control panel. The MM abruptly pitches upright, and the

Martian landscape pivots into view.

He gasps, he can't help himself. He's looking down on a vast desert, reds and umbers and pale browns, from horizon to horizon. It looked so unearthly from orbit, but now, a thousand feet above the surface, it could be Earth, some unvisited corner where dunes creep across the land while sand vortices dance from crest to crest, a landscape punctuated by rocks and hills and ridges. But he knows no one has ever set foot here—he can feel it, a sense of solitude, of desolation, which rises from the Martian soil, is written in the red sand, in the jagged and crumbled escarpments and cliffs.

He thinks, This is it; I'm going to land on Mars, I'm going to be the first man to walk on another planet, I'm in the goddamned history books for sure.

If only Judy could see him now, could feel the same anticipation, the same excitement, the same heightened awareness he now feels, could recognise that this moment *defines* him, that a palpable sense of purpose stretches from this moment, from his heart, both back and forth in time. She'd forgive him for accepting the mission, of course she'd forgive him. He'd told her he was coming back. Again and again, he'd told her he was coming back. Not even one hundred and fifty million miles could keep him from her.

He looks up from the DSKY at the photograph of his wife on the control panel. He will be on Mars for the next nine days, he can talk to Walker, who will be swinging by within one hundred miles of the planet, but Earth is on the other side of the Sun, so there's going to be a long delay on any conversation with Houston. He knows there's been important guests in the MCC throughout the mission, and the viewing gallery will probably be packed with press and VIPs during the nine days of his stay on the surface. Judy will be there, of course. He's looking forward to speaking to her before his first scheduled EVA.

The DPS fires its final burn, and moments later the contact light shines, telling him there's five feet to go, so he

27

braces himself for the landing. The DPS cuts off and the MM drops and hits the surface of Mars with more force than he'd expected. He stumbles and bangs against the control panel, adding another bruise to the ones he's gathered already.

A profound silence fills the MM. He thinks, by God, I did it. I'm on Mars, goddamnit.

He speaks, but his mouth is too dry and all he can make is an unintelligible sound. He tries again, remembering he is speaking to posterity. Houston will not hear his words for thirteen and a half minutes, but this is all part of the script:

Houston, he says, this is Cydonia Base, Discovery has landed.

1999 Before it was captured and bent to NASA's needs, the Robert H Goddard was a Near Earth Asteroid named 1862 Apollo. Peering through the docking windows as the LM Taxi approaches the spacecraft, Elliott sees a grey potato-shaped rock, details unnaturally sharp in the vacuum, smooth and lightly dimpled, just over a mile in length. As the rock rotates beneath him, three white cylinders, resembling the lower stages of rockets on spidery legs and arranged in a triangular formation, roll into view. Two Apollo Command Modules and a single Lunar Module lacking its descent stage are docked to an adaptor on the top of one cylinder; a single Command Module occupies the docking adaptor of another. An area of 1862 Apollo's surface alongside the silo-like modules has been smoothed flat and laid with metal decking. Secured to this decking are three long tubes, which Elliott identifies as launch vehicles in some sort of casing, though he's not sure what type—from the size Atlas Vs, perhaps. He wonders how they managed to get them up into space and out here to the Lagrangian point.

Now that he is closer, Elliott sees the habitation modules have been adapted from S-IVB stages, cylinders forty-eight feet in height and twenty-two feet in diameter. He is surprised: this is old tech. The Ares 9 flyby spacecraft was based on the same hardware, as was the simulator—later known as Skylab and the first station out here at L5. And even back then, the designs were old and their use for Ares 9 more a matter of what was do-able than what was best. He remembers Walker, his CMP on Ares 9, saying they'd flown to the Red Planet as much on political desperation as on Aerozine 50.

Doesn't look like much, does she? says Weber. But she'll take you ninety trillion miles in a couple of weeks.

Where's the Serpo engine? Elliott asks.

Other side of the rock, with the nuclear reactor.

Weber returns her attention to the FDAI and altimeter on the control panel.

They are both in spacesuits, helmets and gloves on. It is procedure when flying a LM Taxi. Elliott spent seventy days in his Mars Module, an uprated LM, and pretty much all of that in his A7LB, so none of this is unfamiliar. True, he had the MM to himself, but here his left arm is inches from Weber's right and he has barely enough room to stretch.

You've flown on her, Elliott asks Weber, to Earth Two?

She shakes her head. No, I'm NASA. It's you guys who fly the Rocks.

Us? Elliott doesn't follow.

USAF. We're strictly passengers, and I've never been assigned to Phaeton Base.

The LM Taxi drops toward the asteroid, then an abrupt shift in his frame of reference hits Elliott and he now sees himself approaching a grey and powdery vertical cliff. The LM Taxi shoots "upward" and he notices Weber is peering up through the docking windows in the roof. Ahead, or above, it no longer matters which, he can see the Goddard's hab modules, like some strange minimalist chemical plant. This is all automatic, computerised, though Weber has still moved the COAS to its mount on the docking window frame and set the panel switch from OFF to OVHD. She keeps her hands on the thrust/translation controller and attitude controller as the docking adaptor drifts nearer. The two tee-crosses, one on the LM Taxi, one on the docking adaptor, gradually line up as the LGC fires tiny corrective bursts from the RCS until, with a thunk, the probe on the Goddard's hatch thumps into the LM Taxi's drogue, and the capture latches engage with a confident crunch.

Once Weber has confirmed the docking tunnel is pressurised, she unfastens her waist restraints and kicks herself upward to the hatch. Moments later, she swings it wide, revealing a man in a blue CWG framed in the hatchway.

Welcome aboard, sir, the man says. With one hand to the coaming to hold him steady, he salutes.

Major William Finley? asks Elliott

It cannot be anyone else. The golden oak leaf on his collar gives the man's rank and Finley, the commanding officer, is the only major on the Robert H Goddard. Finley also has a Space Command shield on one shoulder.

Sir, acknowledges Finley. He pushes himself back, and gestures for Elliott to join him.

I have to head straight back, Weber says. She gives a tight smile. Good luck, she adds; and then pulls herself down to the commander's position and sets about refastening her waist restraints.

Elliott unlocks and then lifts off his helmet. He breathes in through his nose, but the LM Taxi's cabin is odourless. After removing his gloves and dumping them in the upturned bowl of his helmet, he disconnects his spacesuit from the spacecraft's environmental system, and unclips his waist restraints.

Weber ignores him, and stands, a hand to each controller, her expression set, gazing out of the commander's window. It's obvious there's no love lost between the civilian crew of Space Station Freedom and the military crew of the Goddard, and he wonders that such rivalries should exist out here, hundreds of thousands of miles from Earth. He gives a shrug, grabs his kitbag with his free hand and then jumps up towards the docking hatch.

"Up" suddenly becomes "along" and now he's flying toward a hatch on the wall ahead of him. He chucks his kitbag through, grabs the coaming and pulls himself into the docking adaptor. It's a small cubical chamber, and Finley has already moved through another hatch and into what appears to be a much larger space, and is waiting for Elliott to join him.

He does, and once again Elliott's perception shifts: he's now at the top of a wide and deep cylinder with a metal floor composed of triangular gridwork some ten feet below him. Visible through that are another two such floors. He smiles—it looks just like Ares 9, they had that dumb gridwork system too, though they stopped using it less than a week after leaving LEO. Finley drops to the deck, twists one foot then the other, and sticks to the floor. Elliott waits in the hatch and looks around. Up here by the entry hatch, the wall is a ring of lockers. There are more lockers on the top deck, a block of them on the floor to Elliott's left. There is an opening in the centre of the deck giving access to the floor below. It all looks reassuringly familiar.

Elliott pushes himself down to Finley, who reaches out and grabs his arm with a hand about one bicep. He can't feel the major's grip through the layers of his spacesuit. He draws Elliott down until their heads are level.

We'll get you some shoes, Finley tells him.

At that moment, a dull boom shakes the cylinder. Elliott jerks his head up, but Finley appears unconcerned. It is a moment before Elliott realises the noise must have been Weber undocking her LM for the return trip to Space Station Freedom.

Finley leads Elliott down a deck and into a tunnel giving access to the one of the other cylinders. As they pull themselves along, using a rope strung the length of the tunnel, Elliott remarks: Weber told me the Serpo engine is on the other side of the asteroid.

31

Finley glances at him and says, Yeah, in a sealed chamber.

What does it look like? he asks.

Elliott has only the vaguest understanding of how the Serpo engine works—the details are, of course, classified—and he does not recall ever seeing a photograph of it.

No idea, Finley says.

You don't need to maintain it or anything?

Finley gives an amused snort. Us? he says. No, we don't get to do that. Some secret types out of Area 51, they do it. They never take their helmets off and they never lift up their sun visors. None of us has ever seen a single goddamn face of one of them.

They enter the next cylinder and Finley leads the way up to the top deck. This one does not have a hatch in the ceiling, instead there is a cupola, with a window in its top and in each of its six sides. One arc of the module's wall is covered with control panels, and before them two seats are secured to the deck. One of the seats is occupied. A young man, same blue Space Command CWG as Finley, buzz-cut hair, the silver bar of a first lieutenant on his shoulder, glances back as Finley and Elliott appear, but his face does not change expression.

From his briefing back in Houston, Elliott knows the Goddard has a crew of thirteen, organised in three watches: a pilot, flight engineer, navigator and systems engineer on each watch, and the CO.

Finley turns to Elliott and asks, Is it true what they say about the Serpo?

What do they say? Elliott replies.

You command the Flight Test Center at Edwards, right? They say a UFO landed there in '57. Gordo Cooper—you know, one of the Mercury guys—he was there, he saw it. You ever meet Cooper?

Elliott shakes his head. He left NASA three years before I joined, he says.

I heard they pushed him out because of the UFO thing.

Elliott does not immediately reply. What is it with all this flying saucer stuff? True, the Goddard travels faster than the speed of light; but does that mean it has to be little green men? And that the US *stole* faster than light travel from them?

Cooper, he explains, got into a pissing contest with the Astronaut's Office and lost. I heard the scuttlebutt but, you know, it was all kind of academic after Apollo 13.

I heard Cooper had a thing for UFOs, Finley says.

Elliott shrugs. Maybe he did, he replies. I never knew him. They say he was a natural stick and rudder man, best in the programme.

No UFOs then, says Finley. He sounds disappointed.

No UFOs, confirms Elliott; and then he adds, Isn't this science fiction enough for you?

And he swings out an arm to take in the Goddard's command centre and, outside its walls, the asteroid 1862 Apollo and the Earth 250,000 miles away.

1980 Elliott has not moved since the MM landed. He is too busy staring out the window. He has landed due north of the D&M Pyramid and he is staring at an oval-shaped mesa about a mile and half long and half a mile wide, and the same colour as the surrounding landscape. Its side is a sandy slope that looks to have slid and slipped many times. About halfway up the mesa the sand becomes a rocky cliff, weathered and cracked and scoured by dust storms over millions, perhaps billions, of years. But the top of the mesa appears strangely smooth, and smoothly undulating, clear of any outcrops but for a set of sinuous ridges and, in the centre of the mesa's top, a triangular promontory with a long ramp on one side to its peak...

It looks like a face; even from three miles away it looks like a goddamned face.

That pyramid with the ramp is a nose, and just south of

that a pair of curved ridges like lips. North of it there's a deep col like an eyesocket. The Viking 1 photos did not lie. The pencil-necks said it's pareidolia, an accident of lighting and landscape. That isn't really a face on image #35A72. It can't be. There's no intelligent life on Mars, it could never exist there. Mars is a dead world, like the Moon.

Pariedolia or not, the Face was enough to pick Cydonia as the landing site for Ares 9.

He can't see the D&M Pyramid and its mysterious crater since they're behind the MM. But north-west of him he can just make out the region of broken terrain they've nicknamed the "City". It doesn't much resemble ruins from this distance, it's just fractured hills and tumbled rocks and a few dunes and craters.

He may have nine days on Mars but every single moment has been plotted and planned and filled with tasks—though he suspects the view out the window has just made that schedule obsolete. He wants to tell someone what he can see, but there's a protocol for just this contingency: use the code-word to alert Houston, don't mention any of the weird shit, stick to the new mission plan as if it were the original plan and pretend everything is normal.

Sorry about that, Endeavour. You should see the scenery down here. Magnificent!

Great! I heard you all the way down. Going to be a while before Houston gets the message.

Yeah. Let's get this thing safed. I'm going to be here a while, right?

You're good to stay, Discovery.

Let me just find the page on the checklist... Okay, Master Arm on, DPS vent... fire. Master

Arm off. Descent Reg 1 closed...

Yeah, I got it, Bob. Mission Timer open... MGC DSKY open... S-Band antenna open...

Verify cabin pressure... Yup. Cabin Repress on auto. And now I can get this goddamn goldfish bowl off my head.

Next page is circuit breakers—

Okay, copy.

[laughter] You got your first message from Houston scheduled at MET 3124:20:00. That gives you about ten minutes.

This thing's safe as it'll ever be. I think I'll take a rest. Speak to you soon.

The surface gravity here is just over a third of Earth's, but after 130 days in weightlessness it feels like so much more. He unclips his restraint harness and steps back from the commander's position. Just behind him is the box covering the MM's APS. He carefully sits on this, puts his gloved hands on his knees. He wonders about his biosensor telemetry, it's going to look bad to the docs in the MCC. Perhaps they'll put the elevated heartbeat down to excitement, but he bets their consoles won't show how bone-tired he feels. His legs ache, the soles of his feet hurt, he can barely lift his arms and he no longer has the strength to make a fist in his IV gloves. He lets out a long, slow breath and he knows he needs to find some energy from somewhere. He's got to sound chipper, keen, a *proper* astronaut, when he speaks to Houston; he's got to be confident, the living embodiment of the Right Stuff, for Judy. And he's got his first scheduled EVA straight after that. At least with the delay, he'll have time to get his responses just right.

He looks up at the Mission Timer, sees Houston's first contact is about due to arrive, and he wonders where the time went. He's still wearing his helmet, he doesn't think he can remove it right now, and he'd only have to put it back on for the EVA. He's got his microphone set to push-to-talk, so he waits for Capcom's words to cross the Solar System to him...

Discovery, this is Houston. You got a room full of people cheering here. How does it feel to be the first man on Mars? Over.

It feels great, Houston. You know, I landed here, but it won't count for me until I get to put my boot on the surface, and maybe leave a print like Buzz did on the Moon. It won't last as long here, though—a dust storm will wipe it away in week or two. Over.

And now another twenty-seven minutes for his words to cross interplanetary space to Earth, and Houston's reply to fly back. But at least he mentioned Buzz Aldrin, at least he let Houston know that the Face is real.

So what's it like on Mars, Discovery? Everybody here wants to know. I got all the guys, I got the press, I got the guys in the back room, they all want to know. Over.

Okay, I'm looking out the window. In front of the MM the ground is kind of flat and sandy, with small scattered rocks. It's orangey-red, not the sort of colour you see back on Earth. I look up to the horizon and I can see a mesa about three miles away. And off to my right—that's pretty much due north of my position—I can see another mesa. The sky is pale, a sort of pinkish colour at the horizon, probably from the dust, but it turns black real quick as you lift your eyes up.

He steps back and sits down on the APS. He knows he's not doing the landscape justice. Its desolation, the rocks steeped in loneliness, the distant banded hills, the ridges and chaotic terrain... He knows the terminology but he's all too aware they're insufficient, just jargon, incapable of communicating the *sense* of the Martian surface.

You be careful there, Discovery. You're a long way from home. We really want to see Mars for ourselves, so take lots of photographs. And we got someone here wants to speak to you. Over.

Copy that. We've completed the Surface Checklist, so I'm about to get ready for my first EVA. Over.

It isn't going to take him half an hour to get ready for EVA—he already has his spacesuit on, though it isn't pressurised. He needs only to put on his EVA gloves and MEVA, clip his PLSS to his back, and then swap connectors from the MM's air supply to the backpack's. But he waits because he wants to hear from Judy before he exits the MM. He raises a gloved finger to the picture of her on the control panel and presses it gently against the photographic paper. He thinks about how he's going to handle the EVA. At least he doesn't have to worry about television—they don't have the bandwidth to send live pictures back, so he has only a Hasselblad 500 EL and a Maurer 16mm DAC.

Hi, Bradley. Everyone here is really excited you landed on Mars safely. I'm excited too. I know you've trained for this so long, and I know you're going to make us all proud. Be careful for me, darling, and come home safely. Over.

Judy [pause] Judy, I'll be fine here. You keep safe for me. Don't let anyone make you do something if you don't want to do it. I'll be thinking of you all the time here. On Mars. I'll speak to you again after my first EVA. Over.

Elliott switches the O_2 from CABIN to OFF, unplugs the connectors from the front of his spacesuit, and then plugs in the hoses from the PLSS. He backs into the PLSS, manages to get the straps over his shoulder and snaps the buckles into place. He fits the MEVA to his helmet, and then pulls on and locks his EVA gloves. After dumping the air in the cabin, he bends over and rotates the latch handle. The hatch pops off its seal and swings open. Turning about, he struggles down onto his knees and then crawls backwards out onto the MM's porch. He can't bend his knees much in the A7LB, the Martian atmosphere is only 0.087 psi but it might as well be vacuum. He shuffles back until his boots hang over the ladder fixed to the forward landing gear strut. He's practiced this move a dozen times back on Earth, on a full-mock-up of the MM and in the Neutral Buoyancy Laboratory, but he's glad it's only 0.376 G here on Mars. Firmly gripping the railing to either side, he hops back onto the first rung of the ladder.

Moments later, he's on the bottom rung. He stops and looks down. It's only thirty inches to the Martian soil, but this damned spacesuit is heavy and he's already warm from the exertion. He pushes himself off backward, and time seems to slow as he falls towards the red sand. He's looking down, the neckring of his helmet blocking his view of his feet, and he can see the ground drifting closer and closer and closer—

He hits the dirt. There's a billow of orange dust around his boots. Some of it settles on his legs, the rest blows away.

Mankind has just ventured from his home, and there's a whole new world here for us to explore. Let's treat it with respect.

Fine words, Discovery.

I had three months to think of them while we were flying here, Endeavour.

[laughter] I guess I remember that, Discovery.

He moves forward from the MM, describing his surroundings for the folks back on Earth and wishing he had the vocabulary to truly capture the essence of this place. At first sight, Cydonia could be some place on the Colorado Plateau, Monument Valley perhaps, a high desert with mesas and off to his left hills sculpted by millions of years of dust storms set amid broken terrain. But it's also dead, completely lifeless, as if some red poison had settled over the land and killed everything which grew. The ground beneath his feet is hard red rock with a light dusting of red sand. He stamps a foot and watches dust billow out. It travels only a short distance to either side, an inch or two, and then falls fast to the ground. A wisp of red catches a breeze and ghosts off to his left, twisting and writhing before dissipating to nothing.

It's hard work. His spacesuit is heavy, the journey here has weakened him, and he has to fight the A7LB's pressurised bladder with every step. There's not much give in his knees, but he can move his hips and ankles, and he's forced to make small straight-legged skips to move forward, rocking from side to side with each step.

About twenty feet from the MM, he stops. He tries to calm his breathing, he doesn't want to trigger the voice-activated microphone. The Face is about three miles away, just over the horizon, but he can see its upper reaches and though he's seeing it from the side and at lower level, it still doesn't look natural. There's weathering, he can see that now, the tip of the nose is broken and there are cracks on its sides. The ridges which form the lips are broken and a short length is missing completely. He wonders if he hasn't fallen prey to pariedolia himself.

Then he turns around and looks at the MM, crouched in the middle of this desert, its gold skirt smeared with red dust, streaks of orange across the silver planes of its face, and beyond it the D&M Pyramid. And, by God, it looks like a goddamn pyramid. The edges are blurred, the top has collapsed a little, but it looks no more natural than the pyramids of Egypt.

Rested, he heads back to the MM. He jumps up onto the lowest rung of the ladder—it's a struggle, no doubt it was easier on the Moon—and then hops up each rung until he can reach the insulation blanket covering the MRV. He rips it free, pulls off the operating tapes and, lanyard in hand, hops back down the ladder to the surface. Backing away from the MM, he gives the lanyard a yank, and then holds it taut as the Mars Roving Vehicle folds out from its bay, its rear wheels lowering into position and locking, then the front wheels. He shuffles about the vehicle removing pins and cables, then lifts up the seat and footrest.

He steps back and gazes at the MRV. He's done enough for his first EVA, he thinks. Tiredness eats at his bones, his muscles burn, and he can barely bend his fingers in his gloves. It's going to be a fight to get back into the MM, and he best do it now while he's got a chance of succeeding. The mission plan has him out here for another hour, but he's cutting it short.

The mission planners have filled his nine days for him and after forty minutes on Mars he knows there's no way he's going to be able to do everything they want. He's going to have to focus on the important stuff, and he knows the real science is going to get short shrift because another agenda has come into play now. The pencil-necks are going to be pissed at him because other things are more important now—

The goddamn Face. And the Pyramid.

1999 Elliott has been on the Robert H Goddard for a week now and he's fairly sure he knows his way round it. The module through which he came aboard holds supplies, then there's the command module, and the last one is the passenger and crew module. Occasionally he uses the wrong connecting tunnel and finds himself not where he expected to be, but it's pretty easy to figure out which module is which. Everywhere he turns, he is assailed by memories of Ares 9, and they trick him into thinking he knows precisely where he is. And then some strangeness, something that reminds him he's not aboard Ares 9 en route to Mars, he's in the Goddard, travelling to an exoplanet faster than the speed of light.

They've assigned him a compartment, though he had the pick of them as he's the only passenger aboard. They're all exactly the same: a triangular space with a locker against the curved exterior wall and a sleeping bag fastened to an interior partition. A mat on the floor and a canvas ceiling provide privacy.

This tiny compartment where he spends his nights is only a smaller space within a tiny universe. He's cut off from everything outside the Goddard and since he's a passenger he has nothing to do. His thoughts inevitably turn to Judy, and he wonders if he should have contacted her from Space Station Freedom. And then he thinks, no goddamnit, she left him, not the other way round, she's the one who's throwing away their marriage, the years they had together, the good times, the life he created for her. He's not going to apologise, she knew he had to take this mission, he couldn't turn it down, she's the one with the goddamn problem. And he pulls out the photos he brought with him, but it hurts too much to look at them so he puts them away.

He spends most of his time in the command module—the daily operations of the Goddard he finds endlessly fascinating. The crew module has exercise and recreation facilities, and he has to exercise for two hours every day on the ergometer, but he doesn't sleep as well as he once did, not even in zero gravity. The Goddard's crew are mostly young, taciturn, and even off-watch they treat him according to his rank. No one is ever really off duty in space.

Major Finley doesn't seem to mind him hanging around the command centre, providing he stays out of the way. Elliott spends hours in the cupola, gazing out at the surface of 1862 Apollo, which glows silver beneath a nacreous sky.

What is that? he asks Finley, pointing up at the pearly brightness which surrounds the asteroid.

Light, Finley tells him. We're in a bubble of spacetime generated by the Serpo engine, and the light trapped inside with us can't escape until we reach our destination and collapse the bubble, so it just bounces around and produces that effect. When we arrive, it all escapes with a big flash.

The guys on Earth Two say they always know when we arrive—the flash lights up the sky.

It's kind of weird, admits Elliott.

You get used to it, replies Finley. The major floats beside him in the cupola. He glances down at the two officers manning the pilot and flight engineer positions, and then looks across to Elliott. I guess, he says, it's about time you told me what your mission is.

Elliott has been ordered to brief Finley once the Goddard is en route. So he says, About three weeks ago, one of the guys at NASA figured out we should be able to see evidence of Phaeton Base on the L5 Telescope.

Right, says Finley; It's been fifteen years.

Elliott continues, So they watched Gleise 876 for a week and scrutinised the data every which way. Nothing. They expected something, maybe just a shift in the star's spectral lines, maybe a change in brightness—but *something*.

Nothing? Finley scoffs; Did they get the date right?

The date is right. How long since you were last there? Elliott asks.

Maybe three months, admits Finley. We've been doing these supply runs three times a year since they founded the base. Everything's always been pretty normal. You know we had a scheduled trip in three weeks?

Yeah, but this may be urgent. Maybe something happened, it needs checking out. That, says Elliott, is why you're taking me there now.

Finley is plainly not convinced. Why you? he asks. You're not Space Command, you've not been in space for twenty years.

That's classified, Elliott tells him.

Later, Elliott regrets the conversation. Whenever he surprises a member of the Goddard's crew at something, their expression changes when they see him. It's something about himself that causes their features to harden, their brows to lower and eyes narrow. He's seen it before, back at Edwards, when they get some guy through the Test Pilot

School and they can all see he's out of his depth. Elliott knows they're thinking he's the only man to visit Mars, he's some kind of astronaut celebrity, so the brass, maybe even POTUS himself, decided he'd be good for this.

He's in the rec area at the galley table, his feet angled up towards the ceiling, trying to spoon chocolate pudding from a see-through pouch. One of the junior members of the crew, a lieutenant called Stewart, joins him.

They call it Hell, you know, Stewart tells Elliott.

He doesn't understand. The Rock? he asks. The bubble? What?

Earth Two, Stewart replies.

Now that makes sense. Elliott has been studying Earth Two, Gliese 876 d, and it does appear infernal. It's a red globe bathed in red light from its red sun. There are no surface features visible in orbital photographs, only vague lines which hint at mountain ranges, valleys, rifts and plains. The atmosphere hides detail. Pink clouds drift slowly across the hellish landscape, softening the view. Elliott remembers Mars and how every rift and desert and shield volcano was visible from orbit, identifiable from thousands of miles away during his approach.

Is that so, he says.

Stewart nods slyly. They got all the creature comforts there, he says, but they hate it all the same.

What are they doing there? he asks.

Stewart shrugs. Science, he says. Who knows? Science for science's sake. One up on the Russkies, I guess.

1980 The Face was a bust. Three days he drove out to it in the MRV and explored its slopes, but he couldn't find a way up. From some angles, the top of the mesa looks like a real face, with eye-sockets, nose, lips; other times, it just looks like a weathered hill in some pitiless desert. He does not know how old it is, this region was formed during the Amazonian age and is likely three billion years old. At 0.087 psi, a hurricane here is going to feel like a light breeze, it's not going to do much weathering. A mesa like this could be millions of years old on Earth, but here it might be a thousand times older. He doesn't even find any real evidence it's artificial, and that's why they sent him here. There are some cracks between rocks, and maybe they're proof the mesa was put together out of blocks of stone like the Sphinx or something, but they could just as easily be natural. He's not sure, but he has the Hasselblad mounted on his chest so he takes lots of photographs. Let the pencil-necks figure it out.

The City was no better. Two days he spent there, but it's just a jumble of rocks, and if there were any buildings there once it's impossible to tell now. Now he's got two days left on Mars and all this driving around in the MRV has helped a bit but he still feels weak and bone-tired all the time. His spacesuit chafes, he's got some kind of rash that's getting real close to painful, and his hands are black and blue from trying to do things in EVA gloves.

There's only one place he's got left to look: the D&M Pyramid, and it's six miles south of the MM, just over an hour's drive in this terrain in the MRV. He shouldn't go so far, mission protocols say stay within walking distance of the MM, but it's not like he has much choice. He's got to find *something*.

The Pyramid is a good bet because it looks just like one of the pyramids in Egypt. Except it has five sides. The top has been scoured flat by dust storms, and the edges are no longer sharp, but there's no way it can be a natural hill. He pushes the T-bar forward and the MRV picks up speed, throwing out two fine plumes of red dust from its rear wheels. The ground is soft, but at least it's mostly flat, and the wire wheels have more than enough traction so soon he's hitting nearly eight miles per hour. He crests a small dune around three feet high, and bounces down the other side. He's getting the hang of the low gravity now, his reactions are tuned to it. He speeds across the Martian sand and he can't help himself, for the first time since landing here he's feeling happy. The sun is a small white spot, mountains dance in the haze of distance, banded and striped in shades of red and brown and black, and the sky above the horizon is a salmon pink blur. He hits a shallow graben, like an empty stream-bed, and pulls back on the T-bar to reduce speed. If he hits one of those too fast, he'll bust the MRV and it's a *long* walk back to the Mars Module.

Two and a half miles before the Pyramid is a big round crater five or six hundred yards across. He was going to ignore it, drive round it, but now that he's close something about it puzzles him. There's no ejecta, no apron, the rock of the rim is the same basalt as the Pyramid and the surrounding area. He can see no discolouration, no debris where an ejecta blanket should be.

He reaches the rim of the crater—or whatever it is—and brings the MRV to a slewed halt. He unfastens his lap belt but waits a moment before climbing off the vehicle. He's on VOX but none of this conversation is going to get relayed to Houston:

Okay, Bob, I'm at the crater, and it's no crater, man. It's like a collapsed cave or something.

I hope you're taking photos, Brad.

Yeah, but you just know they're going to be classified, right?

[laughter] It's probably natural; it's just you, your mix is just wrong. So what kind of cave?

Could be erosional, I guess, formed back when Mars had water back in the Noachian.

That's four billion years ago,

Brad. That can't be right: Cydonia is Amazonian.

Yeah, I guess. I'm standing on the rim now. I'm seeing banding in the walls, so this is no impact crater. And those walls are way too regular, so it's not erosional either—

You're saying it's artificial?

Yeah, I guess... Wait—

On the Viking 1 image, part of the "crater" floor looked to be in shadow but now he's standing on the lip he can see from edge to edge. And over there, across from him, something glints in a drift against the wall. He looks for a way down—the chamber is about fifty feet deep and sheer-sided—and just around the rim, part of the wall has collapsed, forming a steep slope down. He heads over, kicking up red sand as he bounds across the Martian soil. He weighs 150 pounds here with his spacesuit and PLSS, and that's just over half of what he weighs buck naked on Earth. He reaches the ramp, and steps carefully onto it, placing one boot firmly on the slope, then lifting his foot. For a moment, he admires the bootprint he's made in the red sand, but already grains are spilling in at the edges, blurring its clean lines. He puts his foot down again and his grip feels secure. This ramp has been here for hundreds of thousands of years, maybe longer, the rock and sand is not going to shift from his weight.

Still, he's careful as he descends, but it's steeper than it looks and he starts to lose his balance so he increases his pace and soon he's springing from foot to foot down the ramp, always about to topple over, only just in control—

You okay, Brad?

I'm... shit... steep... steeper... than... I thought... shit... Okay, I'm at the bottom now. Damn, that was stupid.

I'm on the floor. I saw
something, I'm going to check
it out.

Bottom of what, Brad?

He heads across the floor of the—yes, it's a chamber, a *built* thing, carved from the rock. He's hot and his ankles ache and the soles of his feet are sore from descending the ramp at speed. He shuffles across the sandy red rock, scuffing through the drifts of sand, rocking from side to side, and it's hard work. He can see the glint more clearly now, and once he's within a dozen feet of it he sees it's a curved fragment of transparent mineral. It's too big to be natural, he thinks, but with the Face and now this underground chamber, he's lost all sense of surprise.

He bends forward, preventing himself from falling over with a hand to the drift, and tries to dig away at it. But the transparent thing, whatever it is, it's buried deep in the rock, and he can't get it out. All he does is bruise his fingertips badly in the thimbles of his gloves, and he has to bite back an oath at the pain. He wonders if it's worth getting it out, but just then some of the rock crumbles and falls away and he can see a bit more of the sheet and—

There's something inside it.

It's black and thin and curved, but he can't see more than that. It's like a tiny black worm maybe, or a tail of some small creature. He's got a geology hammer but he left it on the MRV. He's going to need it now.

He heads back across the floor, scrambles up the ramp, and by the time he reaches the top, he has to stop to cool down. After ten minutes, he's got his breath back and he thinks he can move without danger of heat exhaustion. He shuffles over to the MRV, grabs the hammer and the sampling scoop from the Hand Tool Carrier behind the seat, and then returns to the floor of the chamber.

He's sweating and swearing again as he hammers at the

rock to uncover more of the transparent whatever. He's hit it several times with the hammer by accident and it hasn't even scratched it. He thinks it may be diamond. A giant diamond. On Mars.

It takes him a couple of hours but soon he has most of the diamond dug out. It's a disc about six feet in diameter and three inches thick, and it's covered in writing, small symbols about two inches square in a spiral from the edge into the centre. They're *inside* the diamond, and they're not human. They can't be—this rock the sheet is buried in is millions of years old. And if this is a hoax, then Major Bradley Emerson Elliott, USAF, is not the first human being on Mars, and he's pretty damn sure he is. Besides which, no one on Earth can make a huge diamond like this.

He peers closer at the symbols and he sees there are two separate spirals. One of them tells a story in little pictograms, with little planets and stars and lines connecting them every which way. He thinks one planet is Mars, and it's connected by a line to another that could be the Earth but has only one big continent. It also has a line of symbols by it, then there's a line from some constellation he doesn't recognise to the Earth; and now here's the Earth again but the symbols have gone. And another line to Mars where there's a little drawing of the Face, and even a tiny pictogram of this disc...

He takes photos, lots of photos. They're going to want to see this back at Houston. His camera runs out of film, and he thinks he should start back to the MM. He looks at his Omega Speedmaster and over four hours have passed. He's got plenty of time, the PLSS is good for a seven-hour EVA and it's about an hour's drive back to the MM. But it's definitely time he got going.

He leaves the hammer and sampling scoop and crosses to the ramp up to the rim. Exhaustion limits his actions. He moves like an old man, he's covered in a thin film of sweat and the LCG can't keep him cool enough. If he stands still too long, he can feel sleep begin to steal upon him, and it takes an effort of will to remain awake and moving.

It takes him far too long to ascend out of the chamber, but eventually he makes it to the top, and he has to rest for twenty minutes. Once he has recovered, he makes his way slowly to the MRV and settles gratefully into its seat. He fastens the lap-belt, grabs the T-bar and pushes it forward. He's tired, he's not thinking straight. The MRV spins its wheels and then lurches forward. Too late, he thinks to pull the T-bar towards him. The front left wheel hits a rock, the entire vehicle bounces, and when it hits the ground, the wheel is bent out of true.

Elliott's mind blanks. He sits there and gazes at the MRV's broken wheel. This vehicle's not going to move any further, and it's a four mile hike back to the MM. For the first time since launching from the Cape, since arriving on Mars, he feels real fear. He puts the MRV in reverse and gently pushes the T-bar forward, but it's not going to work, that bent wheel just jams against the chassis. Maybe he could fix it with the hammer, but he left the hammer down by the alien disc and he's not sure he has the strength to go up and down that ramp again. Nor does he have the time to spare trying to fix the MRV.

He has to walk.

He clambers off the MRV and turns until he faces due north. He can't see the MM, it's over the horizon. He can't even see the Face. Just a red desert of low dunes, scattered rocks, striped and scalloped hills in the distance blurred by a pink haze beneath a pastel sky. He's used to the red now, it's like his eyes are filtering it out and for one brief moment he sees an Earthly desert and he forgets he's weighed down by an A7LB and PLSS. It's almost as if he can feel a hot sun beating down on him and his mouth turns dry at the thought of it. There's the track through the sand he made when he drove here. He just needs to follow that. He can do it, it's only three and a half, maybe four, miles, he's got three hours of air left in the PLSS.

He starts walking, but how it hurts. This spacesuit has

no range of movement in the knee, it's all in the hips and ankles. He's used to it, but it's hard work, the 0.367 G is no help, and after a week on Mars his muscles ache almost constantly. Soon he's on autopilot, his mind drifts off somewhere, he moves his legs but he's not conscious of doing so. His ankles are sore, his hips ache, his bruised hands pain him, it's like he can feel his bones grating against one another. The MRV is now so far behind him now he can't see it, he's surrounded by lifeless desert and he shuffles through it like it's the spacesuit doing the walking and not the man inside it.

The excitement of his discovery has gone, blown away, and he's so weak now he doesn't know if he can keep on moving. It's like walking on fire with broken ankles and hips. The red sand is a bed of flames, he's so hot he's starting to boil, he's walked so far he's walked clean off Mars and into Hell. He's not going to make it, he's going to collapse in the sand, he'll never make it to the MM. Tears run down his cheeks and he slides one foot forward and then the other. He closes his eyes and he can see Judy. She's standing in front of the French windows and she glows with light like an angel. It's the photograph he has back in the MM, it's there in front of him, just out of reach. No, *she* is just out of reach, and she's beckoning him to her. He roars through the pain, he can't lift his arms to embrace her, but he stumbles on, drawn toward the presence of her, the light of her...

1999 Elliott is in the cupola when the Robert H Goddard arrives at Gliese 876. The pearly shell which encloses the asteroid abruptly vanishes and the universe rushes in, a sudden blackness which leaves spots before his eyes. Then a river of stars spreads across the sky in an eyeblink as if thrown by some Jackson Pollock of the heavens.

Gliese 876 is a dim red furnace about two million miles

distant. The Goddard rotates, and Gliese 876 d, Earth Two—Hell—rolls into view. It's a huge world, three times the size of Earth, and it just plain *looks* hot. Beneath the crimson light of its sun, the land resembles a planet-spanning brushfire, the edges of hills and valleys limned in blood-red. He's seen the PBS specials, but the one thing those shows can't capture is the world's sheer presence. There is nothing like it in the Solar System—it's as barren as the Moon, but it has air and clouds and a climate. And that red light...

Up near the north pole, where Phaeton Base is located, they say it's like a hot day in north Africa. Elliott is not convinced. Surface gravity is 1.5G—that and the red light is not going to feel like Africa to him. He's been told he'll get used to it.

He somersaults and dives down from the cupola. Another somersault as he approaches the deck, and he hits it with both feet and locks the triangular cleats on his shoes into the gridwork.

Finley is standing behind the pilot and flight engineer, one hand on the back of the pilot's chair. His other hand he has up to one of the earpieces in his communications cap and he is talking slowly and clearly into his microphone, saying, Phaeton Base, this is the Robert H Goddard, please respond.

Elliott glances across at Stewart at the navigator's station. No response? he asks.

We can't even find the damn base on the remote telescope, Stewart replies. He grimaces. Can't get the radio beacon either, he adds.

This is what Elliott was sent here to investigate. And it looks like Phaeton Base really has vanished. But if it has disappeared, where has it gone? And what caused the disappearance?

Later they gather round the galley table in the rec area. A pilot and flight engineer remain on duty in the command centre, but everyone else is here. It's crowded. The table can only comfortably fit six, so the other six are scattered about the area at different heights and in different orientations. Elliott is at the table, shoes firmly cleated to the deck. He's sort of in charge.

The base is not responding, Finley says, not on S-Band or VHF.

From four hundred miles up, the base should be visible. They keep it brightly-lit at all times—the dim red sunlight badly affects morale. There is also an extensive greenhouse, and that splash of green would certainly stand out against the relentless red of Earth Two's surface.

I don't get it, says one of the systems engineers, McKay.

You think maybe it's aliens? asks Stewart. He looks pointedly at Elliott, and adds, That's why they sent you, right? You've been to Area 51, you've seen aliens there. Right?

There are no aliens and no UFOs at Area 51, Elliott responds. He holds up a hand, and continues, But that doesn't mean we can't rule out an extraterrestrial cause here. We're fifteen light years from Earth, after all.

That last fact means they're on their own. There's no way of communicating with Earth. A radio message would take fifteen years to reach home, assuming they had equipment powerful enough.

I have to go down there, Elliott says. Maybe there's clues on the ground to what happened.

Too dangerous, replies Finley.

Dangerous? scoffs Elliott; It's a dead world. Fifteen years we've had a base there and they've found zip.

Yeah, but now the base is gone. Maybe they *did* find something, maybe that's what happened to the base.

All the more reason for me to go down there, insists Elliott.

The rest watch impassively as he and Finley argue it out. The major may command the Goddard, but this is Elliott's mission and he knows it. Elliott calls the shots.

Goddamnit, Finley snaps. Why? Going down there is

dumb. If you can't find the base, there's no way back up.

We have to know what happened, Elliott says mulishly.

Is this why they picked you for this mission? Finley sneers.

That's classified, Elliott says.

And that's it: argument over. Finley has no comeback to that. Reluctantly, he agrees to Elliott's plan. One of the flight engineers is sent to prep a Command Module for a descent. They will also load it with plenty of supplies.

Elliott returns to his compartment to dress in his spacesuit. He floats beside the sleeping bag attached to the wall. From his PPK, he pulls out a photograph of his wife and gazes at it. This is not the picture he took to Mars. A couple of years ago, he and Judy visited the Grand Canyon, and he snapped this photo in the car park by the Hopi House. He remembers telling Judy about Valles Marineris, and though he never visited the Martian canyon it struck him he's as much an historical artefact as the Hopi House. He's the only man on Earth who can talk about Mars and its scenery as someone who has visited there.

In the photograph, Judy is smiling, and it's one of her rare unguarded smiles. He married her because of that smile—something during her childhood, she never told him what, made her wary and undemonstrative as an adult. But sometimes he surprised her in a display of real happiness, and he treasured those rare genuine smiles. He profoundly regrets he did not make her happy more often. During his darker days, and he has them like anyone else, he wonders if he would have sacrificed Mars for those smiles.

He's not spoken to her for over a month, not since leaving the house for the Cape, and this photograph is the only one he has. When he went to Mars, they spoke regularly, and her voice kept him going during those 667 days travelling through emptiness. Later, she admitted she'd hated every minute she'd spent in the public eye, hated her own complicity in the media circus, hated herself for believing she was doing it out of loyalty to her husband,

54

and to NASA. One night, she even confessed she'd believed she needed to be loyal to safeguard him during the mission. He has never told her about his long walk back to the MM after he broke the MRV, he has never said how close he came to dying on Mars. It was a poor reward for her loyalty, his dishonesty. But she's not loyal now, she's probably already packed up and left. Perhaps he deserves it.

He shoves some clothes into his kitbag and dresses quickly in his spacesuit. He returns to the rec area on the deck above, where Finley waits for him. The major leads him up to the docking adaptor at the top of the module, where the hatch to one of the Command Modules gapes wide. Elliott swims into the CM and brings himself to a halt on the bank of seats. Turning about, he sees Finley hovering in the open hatch.

You sure about this? the major asks.

Elliott nods. He pulls himself about and, holding onto the seat's struts, pushes himself down until his rear touches canvas. It's a struggle to get the harness fastened, and so Finley enters the CM to give him a hand. This involves the major putting a foot to Elliott's chest and pressing him down and then clipping the harness together and tightening the straps. Elliott says nothing about the triangular cleat on Finley's sole pressing into his sternum, though it's painful. It feels like the pain is deserved.

Crossfield has loaded up the landing program, Finley says as he returns to the hatch; You shouldn't have to do anything.

Thanks, says Elliott.

There's also a radio with the food and water and oxygen in the Lower Equipment Bay. You'll not want to wear your spacesuit down there, it's pretty damn hot.

They told me to pack some light clothes, Elliott replies.

Finley laughs. Yeah, he says, Light clothes. He has reached the hatch. He exits, turns about and peers back in. If you want, he says, we can parachute you down an Atlas V. It's no good to you without a launch pad but, hell, we got boosters to spare.

Elliott shakes his head. If I need one, he replies, I'll let you know. Let me see what it's like on the ground first.

Fair enough, Finley says. He pauses a moment, and then adds, Godspeed. If you find them, it could be one day I can say I met the first man to meet aliens.

Even if I don't find them, says Elliott, you can still tell people that and it'll be true.

1981 In Moscow, the First Man on Mars meets the First Man on the Moon. They shake hands and exchange pleasantries through interpreters for the watching dignitaries and press. Alexei Arkhipovich Leonov is courteous but guarded. Later, over vodka and caviar, through an English-speaking comrade, Leonov confesses that the lunar landing instruments in his LK threw a persistent error.

I make manual landing, he tells Elliott.

Elliott wonders what would have happened if Leonov had aborted and Armstrong had not. An American would have been the First Man on the Moon.

He toasts the Soviet cosmonaut, and glances across the room at his wife. Judy is speaking to a handsome and well-dressed woman with carefully-coiffured brown hair. It is a moment before he identifies her as Valentina Tereshkova, the first woman in space.

And over there, Bob Walker is talking—via an interpreter—to Oleg Grigoryevich Makarov, the LOK pilot for the second Soviet lunar landing. Bob's wife, Valerie, is by his side, one arm hooked through his.

This world tour has been hard, but it has been good for the Elliott marriage. The Ares programme almost killed it. Days smiling for the camera, pills every night or she could not sleep. She came so very close to walking away; she has made that abundantly clear to him.

But travelling about the world, parades in every major

city, meeting important people, seeing the sights: it's been... fun. The interminable receptions and banquets, the endless parade of self-important faces—perhaps not. But in the moments they've stolen from their busy schedule, they have rediscovered each other.

They have visited Mexico City, Buenos Aires, Rio de Janiero, Madrid, Paris, Amsterdam, Oslo, West Berlin, London, Rome, Ankara, Kinshasa, and now Moscow. It has been hectic but at least they are travelling in style: the President has lent them one of his Boeing VC-137C airliners. Elliott refers to it jokingly as "Air Force One", though it uses that callsign only if the President is aboard.

Elliott feels profoundly grateful, and not just to the President and NASA. He's not only lucky to be here, he's lucky to be alive— No, not luck. It wasn't luck that got him back to the Mars Module after he broke the wheel on the MRV. He did it himself. He was on reserve air by the time he reached the MM, and he spent his last day on Mars too tired and in too much pain to do anything but lie in his hammock. Then there was the 537-day free-return trip to Earth—and once the high from reaching Mars had gone and the boredom set in, he and Walker carefully avoiding each other, trying to find a way to live together in such close confines during those long days drifting through the lifeless dark, conflicted by disappointment at the mission's imminent end and a yearning for home and an end to this limitless night...

Re-entry. Splashdown. Lying in their seats unable to cope with Earth gravity. Weak and wasted from over two years in freefall. They had to lift the CM onto the deck of the recovery ship while he and Walker remained inside.

And as soon as they had recovered, off they were sent on this round-the-world press junket.

Afterwards, back in the US, Elliott returns to his military career. Given what he discovered on Mars, the government wants him out of the public eye. Although he's the only human being to have set foot on an alien world, he is quietly asked to retire from NASA and go back to the Air Force. By 1983, Elliott is flying F-15s out of Ramstein Air Base, Germany. Judy loves Europe. She no longer likes being an Air Force wife, but she can't get enough of the "old world" charm of nearby German towns like Saarbrücken, and she frequently visits further afield in Europe.

Elliott has imagined the space programme would gradually wind down now that NASA has met its objective. And so it does for a couple of years. There's still the flyby simulator, now dubbed "Skylab", still in orbit and continually manned. It even has a space telescope fitted to it. But then there's a flurry of activity, more Saturn Vs ordered, North American and Grumman with full order books, and Skylab is moved out to one of the Earth-Moon Lagrangian points. It's used as a staging post to a Near-Earth Asteroid, which is captured and returned to L5. Elliott makes quiet enquiries about returning to NASA—this stuff sounds real interesting and he wants to be involved—but he's firmly rebuffed.

Each year, Elliott is visited by agents from the NSA, who remind him of the consequences should he discuss the Cydonia Codex, which is what they're calling the disc with the alien writing on it. Five years after the mission, they tell him scientists working at Area 51 have had a breakthrough and Elliott has done his country a service it can never repay.

In 1988, the President reveals the US has a manned base on an exoplanet and has been making secret test flights to nearby stars for four years. A NSA agent confirms to Elliott the faster than light engine came out of Area 51 and was based on the maths on the photos of the disc Elliott brought back from Mars.

Elliott is deeply disappointed at what he has missed. His achievement, landing on Mars, the only man ever to do so, feels as though it has been trivialised, as though the giant step he made has been rendered foolish and of no consequence.

58

Perhaps Pete Conrad felt the same on the day Elliott stepped down from the MM.

The interstellar test flights announcement results in a fight with Judy. She leaves him, and it is a week before he learns she has gone to Paris. She rents a small apartment in the 20th arrondissement, and does not return for two months.

In 1989, Bob Walker dies of cancer after a long, protracted illness. His doctors are unanimous in blaming the flight to Mars as the cause. Though Elliott undergoes regular checks, his health remains good. Whatever stray cosmic ray triggered cancer in Walker, it missed Elliott.

In 1993, Elliot is promoted to brigadier general and given command of the Air Force Flight Test Center at Edwards AFB. He and Judy settle in California for what they imagine will be the twilight of Elliott's career. Humanity has visited the stars—thanks to Elliott, though he received no credit for it—and found the universe wanting. More than a decade after the first interstellar flight, there is still only a single US scientific station on an exoplanet, a world orbiting the star Gliese 876 fifteen light years from Earth. The universe has been revealed as a pitiless and hellish place, too dangerous and expensive and difficult to exploit—at least for the time-being, given current American technology.

Elliott's mission to Mars is all but forgotten, mentioned only on PBS science programmes, public access shows about UFOs and the Face on Mars, or in nostalgic sci-fi novels. He has almost forgotten it himself; he is a career military officer now, and feels as though he always has been. The 130 days he spent in space, hurtling between the Earth and Mars, the nine days on the Martian surface, the 537-day return flight—they might never have happened.

He loves flying, he has always loved flying; and as commander of the Flight Test Center he gets to fly whatever and whenever he wants. But some days he sits at his desk and hears another muffled roar as somewhere in the distance a F-5E or a B-52 takes off, and he remembers sitting atop a Saturn V as far below him five F-1 rocket engines ignite, their basso profondo roar, their infernal power pushing him faster and faster and faster. He remembers days spent in an Apollo Command Module and a hab module made out of a S-IVB, he recalls the descent to Cydonia in the MM. He wishes he had been allowed to stay an astronaut, to perhaps work on the interstellar spacecraft USAF now operates.

And then one day, the phone on his desk rings and a voice tells him General Sheldrake P Williams, commander of Air Force Space Command, would like to speak to him. And the first question the general asks him is:

How'd you like to go back into space again?

2000 It has been nearly twenty years since Elliott last experienced splashdown, though strictly speaking this is not a "splashdown" as Earth Two possesses no surface water. He is briefly amused that his first, Ares 3, was as pilot of a crew of three; for Ares 9 he was commander of a crew of two; and now he is on his own in the CM. He ignores the empty seats to either side of him, and gazes at the control panel as if he's actually in command of this flight.

It's a fierce ride. The air is thicker here and the atmosphere deeper. G-forces press him into his seat, he thinks maybe eight or nine G, and it's an effort to remain silent under the strain. He's still a physically fit man, he needs to stay in shape to fly high-performance jets, but this is hard work. He only remembers one time before when everything has been such an effort, and that was during his nine days on Mars. Streaks of flame, yellow and red, stream past out the window, and then it's all white-hot enveloping fire. He watches the altimeter and tries to remember the numbers Finley gave him just before he left the Goddard. It doesn't matter much—the AGC has been programmed for

Earth Two landings, he's just a passenger.

The CM rolls over 180 degrees on schedule and he knows he won't be bounced off the atmosphere. The Gs start to drop and a great weight lifts from his chest. He pulls in a grateful breath. The spacecraft rolls this way and that, lining itself up for the landing. It's freefalling now, and he glances at the Mission Timer and waits for the 16½-feet diameter drogue chutes to be released. A thump, and there they go. The CM jerks and slows and steadies. A long anticipatory moment of silence. Now the main chutes deploy with a bang, and the CM seems to slow until, slow seconds later, the reef lines are cut and the mains chutes open to their full diameter of 83½ feet and it feels like he's hit a brick wall. Elliott bites off a cry of pain. The spacecraft is still dropping, but slowly, and swinging ponderously from side to side.

Ten feet above the ground, the retro-engines—added for landings on the waterless exoplanet—fire and the CM settles with a roar and a thump on the surface of Earth Two. Elliott remains in his seat. He's feeling weak from almost three weeks in zero gravity, and the G forces he experienced on the way down have near drained him.

After ten minutes, he feels recovered enough to attempt an exit. He unlocks and removes his helmet and then his IV gloves. He unbuckles his harness and pushes the straps from his torso. He's lying on his back at about a thirty degree angle, so he hitches his rear back until he is sitting upright. Getting from there down into the Lower Equipment Bay without banging arms or knees on struts or lockers or control panel takes care. He nearly does it, but by the time he's got his breathing mask on, and an oxygen bottle on a sling about his neck, he's nursing a bruise on one shin. He clambers across to the hatch and yanks down the pump handle. There's a hiss as gas is forced from the bottles, the gears grind, and the hatch pops open and swings wide.

Despite the mask, a smell of burnt earth and hot metal

immediately fills the CM. Elliott finds himself short of breath and it takes an effort of will to slow and deepen his breathing. He scrambles out of the hatch and he's standing on the surface of Earth Two and—

This is not Earth and it's not Mars. He is in the middle of a plain of dark rocky soil. It looks almost purple. The sky is red, fading to black at the zenith, and the only light is a dim crimson that washes like blood over everything. On the horizon, he can make out a low range of hills, looking almost pink in the distance. The horizon itself strangely seems to curve slightly upwards.

After fetching his kit from inside the CM, Elliott strips off his spacesuit and dresses in suitable clothing: sturdy trousers, hiking boots, thin shirt. It's very warm, almost tropical but for the dryness. It reminds him of a trip into the Arizona desert, back when he was training for Ares 9. He can feel the skin of his forearms puckering from heat and the lack of moisture in the air.

The CM has landed due south of Phaeton Base. The surrounding landscape is empty and dead, entirely desolate, but there's a ridge to the north, forming the upcurved horizon, and the base ought to be in that direction. It's difficult to judge distance here, but the ridge looks to be about three miles away. An hour's walk, perhaps more given the gravity is about half again what he's used to. He settles his rucksack on his back and sets off.

Elliott stands atop the ridge and looks down into the valley where Phaeton Base should have stood. He sees a gently-sloped declivity, red like everything in this infernal landscape, an expanse of the same powdery soil that is beneath his boots. There is no sign of the base, of its dozen buildings, the great shed that was the rocket assembly building, not even any scorched ground where once the launching pad had been.

He starts forward, walking slowly down the hill. Has the base been removed? Its buildings were on stilts, but he can't even see any disturbed soil. He's not precisely sure where in this valley Phateon Base was located, but it's somewhere around here. He spots something on the ground ahead, a hole perhaps, and increases his pace. But it's only a small dark rock, half-buried in the soil.

Thirty minutes later, he's explored the ground on which Phaeton Base stood, but has found no evidence it ever existed. The soil is completely undisturbed.

He takes off his rucksack, and pulls out the radio from a side-pocket. It's pre-set to the frequency used by the Goddard and, according to his watch—the same Omega Speedmaster he took to Mars—the spacecraft should be overhead. He plugs the radio into the mike jack on his mask, and reports in. Finley answers:

Reading you loud and clear, sir.
What have you found?

> Nothing. If it was ever here, there's no evidence I can find.

You're in the right place?

To prove it, Elliott pulls a flare from his rucksack, lights it and then sticks it upright in the ground. It burns fiercely, too bright to look at even in this dim redness.

Yeah, we got you on the remote telescope. The coordinates match. It's definitely gone then?

> Like it was never here.

No aliens?

> [laughter] No *life*.

I guess that's it then.

> How long are you going to hang around for?

Another week, maybe. You got about a month's worth of supplies, right? It's a damn shame it had to be one-way—

I knew what I was doing. You
can rest easy on that score. I
knew I'd be stuck down here.

Yeah, well. It was an honour to
meet you, sir.

They sent Elliott to Earth Two because he is the only
astronaut who knows for a cold hard fact there is life
elsewhere in the universe. He is the only man to have seen
the evidence. It was just a disc covered in alien writing and
it was billions of years old, but he knows it was real because
it gave the US the Serpo engine. He wouldn't be here now
on an exoplanet orbiting Gliese 876 if it hadn't been real.

But he doesn't think aliens have done this, he doesn't
think the disappearance of Phaeton Base was caused by
aliens. Brigadier General Bradley Elliott, USAF, lifts a hand
to his brow and gazes toward the setting sun. As Gliese 876
falls on the hills lining the horizon, streaks of blood-red
spread out across the bottoms of clouds, and he can't help
thinking it may be an omen. The light creates a bowl of
hues across the sky, mauve above the horizon, through
carmine, crimson, ruby, amaranth and magenta. The
topmost layer, a pale coral colour, fades away to black. The
temperature has dropped but it's still very warm. He's not
going to freeze tonight. Or any night.

It's dark now, the profound darkness that exists only in
deserts far from light pollution. Some stars have appeared
and their light is enough to see by. They sparkle like
diamonds, flashing and blinking, *scintillating*. It's a weird
effect, an *alien* effect. Elliott unrolls his sleeping bag and
lays it on the ground. This world is dead, there is nothing
that can do him injury while he sleeps. He has more than
enough oxygen in his bottle, and a spare in the rucksack
should it run out. Despite the discomfort of the mask, he
falls asleep quickly, and only wakes when red sunlight
creeps across the land. He is hungry and very thirsty.

After a chocolate bar and plenty of water, he packs up

his sleeping bag, shrugs his rucksack onto his back, and returns to the CM. Once he has loaded himself up with supplies, he will start walking. Any direction is as good as another. He has enough food and water and oxygen to last him a while yet. He turns and scans the crimson sky, trying to figure out where Earth is. At fifteen light years' distance, the Sun is just another star. When he thinks he's looking in the right direction, he mouths a silent farewell to Judy.

This time, he is not going home.

APPENDICES

GLOSSARY

Apollo 1 Intended to be the first manned Apollo mission, it never left the launch-pad when a fire in the Command Module during a plugs-out test resulted in the deaths of all three crew. Crew: Virgil 'Gus' Grissom (CDR), Edward H White (senior pilot) and Roger Chaffee (pilot).

Apollo 4 to 6 These three launches were unmanned tests of the hardware: the Saturn V launch vehicle, Lunar Module and Command Module.

Apollo 7 This was the first manned Apollo mission, although it used a Saturn IB as a launch vehicle rather than the Saturn V needed for missions to lunar orbit. The crew spent eleven days in LEO. Crew: Walter M Schirra (CDR), Walter Cunningham (LMP) and Donn Eisele (CMP). Command Module no callsign (CM-101). Launched 11 October 1968.

Apollo 8 Rumours of a possible Soviet attempt to send a cosmonaut round the Moon, and the delay of a Lunar Module for testing in LEO, prompted NASA to re-task Apollo 8 and send it to orbit the Moon. This made its crew the first human beings to leave Earth orbit. Crew: Frank Borman (CDR), William Anders (LMP) and James Lovell (CMP). Command Module no callsign (CM-103). Launched 21 December 1968.

Apollo 9 The first Apollo mission with a Lunar Module, and so tasked with testing rendezvous and docking procedures between the two spacecraft in LEO. Crew: James McDivitt (CDR), Russell 'Rusty' Schweickart (LMP) and David Scott (CMP). Callsigns: Command Module Gumdrop (CM-104), Lunar Module Spider (LM-3). Launched 3 March 1969.

Apollo 10 A "dry run" mission for the first lunar landing, Apollo 10 flew to the Moon and its Lunar Module descended to within ten miles of the lunar surface but did not land. Crew: Thomas P Stafford (CDR), Eugene Cernan (LMP) and John Young (CMP). Callsigns: Command Module Charlie Brown (CM-106), Lunar Module Snoopy (LM-4). Launched 18 May 1969.

Apollo 11 Despite losing the race to the Soviets, NASA continued with its plan to put two men on the Moon. Apollo 11, the third lunar mission, was intended to make the first landing, but a repeating 1202 error during the descent in the Lunar Module forced Armstrong to abort three hundred feet above the lunar surface. The LM returned to the Command Module and, after a further day in lunar orbit, the spacecraft returned to Earth. Crew: Neil A Armstrong (CDR), Edwin E 'Buzz' Aldrin (LMP) and Michael Collins (CMP). Callsigns: Command Module Columbia (CM-107), Lunar Module Eagle (LM-5). Launched 16 July 1969.

Apollo 12 The fourth lunar mission and the first American spacecraft to land on the Moon, at Oceanus Procellarum. Crew: Charles 'Pete' Conrad (CDR), Alan L Bean (LMP) and Richard F Gordon (CMP). Callsigns: Command Module Yankee Clipper (CM-108), Lunar Module Intrepid (LM-6). Launched 14 November 1969, landed on Moon 19 November 1969. Duration on lunar surface 31h 31m 12s.

Apollo 13 This mission failed to complete after an explosion in an oxygen tank in the Service Module. The Lunar Module was successfully used as a lifeboat, and returned the crew to Earth. As a result of the disaster, further trips to the Moon were shelved, and NASA began working on a mission to Mars. Crew: James A Lovell (CDR), Fred W Haise (LMP) and John 'Jack' Swigert (CMP). Callsigns: Command Module Odyssey (CM-109), Lunar Module Aquarius (LM-7). Launched 11 April 1970.

Area 51 A military base in southern Nevada some eighty miles north-west of Las Vegas. It was originally built for the development and testing of the Lockheed U-2 spy plane during the 1950s, expanded during the 1960s for the Lockheed A-12/SR-71 Blackbird programmes, and thereafter associated solely with highly-classified military aviation projects. It has been the subject of numerous conspiracy theories involving Unidentified Flying Objects and reverse-engineered alien technology, none of which have ever been officially confirmed.

Other names for the base include Dreamland, Paradise Ranch and Groom Lake.

Ares 1 After the cancellation of Apollo, the remaining seven Saturn V launch vehicles were transferred across to the Ares programme. Existing hardware was quickly re-engineered and by early 1974, Ares 1 was ready to launch. It put into LEO a S-IVB which had been modified into a "dry workshop" as per a design drawn up ten years earlier. This flyby spacecraft simulator, later known as the "Orbital Workshop", would remain a base for the Ares programme throughout the next five years before eventually being re-purposed and renamed "Skylab". Crew: John Young (CDR), T Kenneth Mattingly (pilot) and Charles Duke (science pilot). Launched 3 May 1974.

Ares 2 This mission put a CSM and LM in orbit in order to test docking and rendezvous procedures with the flyby spacecraft simulator. Crew: Eugene Cernan (CDR), Ronald E Evans (pilot) and Robert F Walker (science pilot). Launched 18 September 1974.

Ares 3 The first of two missions to test the habitability of the flyby spacecraft simulator. The three crew spent a total of 84 days in orbit and performed a number of valuable experiments on Closed Environmental Life Support Systems. Crew: Charles 'Pete' Conrad (CDR), Bradley E Elliott (pilot) and Joseph P Kerwin (science pilot). Launched 31 January 1975.

Ares 4 The last test mission for the Ares programme, its crew of three spent eighteen months aboard the spacecraft flyby simulator in order to verify its long-term habitability. Crew: Alan L Bean (CDR), Jack R Lousma (pilot) and Owen Garriott (science pilot). Launched 15 October 1977.

Ares 5 to 7 In order to reach the required velocity for its journey to Mars, the Ares 9 stack required three S-IVB stages for its Mars Orbit Injection burns. The launches were made in quick succession since the LOX/LH2 fuel was only viable for sixty days in orbit before boil-off reduced it to levels inadequate for the mission. The crews aboard the CSMs built the Ares 9 stack and remained in orbit until its departure. Crews: Ares 5, David Scott (CDR), Gerald P Carr (pilot) and Edward Gibson (science pilot); Ares 6, Thomas P Stafford (CDR), Vance D Brand (pilot) and Donald K 'Deke' Slayton (science pilot); and Ares 7, Richard F Gordon (CDR), Paul J Weitz (pilot) and Don L Lind (science pilot). Launched 27 September 1979, 3 October 1979 and 14 October 1979.

Ares 8 The first part of the manned portion of the Ares 9 stack, carrying the Mars Module and the heatshield needed for the MM to land on the Martian surface. The heatshield was carried to orbit folded and needed to be extended and then its adaptor bolted to the descent stage of the MM. Like Ares 5 through 7, the crew remained in orbit until Ares 9's departure. This put fourteen astronauts in LEO at the same time, the most people in orbit at one time by the US or USSR up to that point. Crew: Fred W Haise (CDR), Stuart A Roosa (pilot) and William R Pogue (science pilot). Launched 28 October 1979.

Ares 9 The first, and to date only, manned mission to Mars. It was based on the Flyby-Landing Excursion Mode mission, using upgraded spacecraft originally built for Apollo lunar landings. The Ares 9 launch put into LEO the mission's CSM and flyby spacecraft, a modified S-IVB, improved after lessons learned operating the Ares 1 flyby simulator. Once the stack had been bolted together, it was boosted on a conjunction-class mission, with a free-return trajectory, to the Red Planet. Thirty days out from Mars, the Mars Module – an uprated Lunar Module, strengthened and provisioned, and with a crew of one – undocked and continued on alone to Mars and a landing on the surface. The Ares flyby spacecraft passed within 150 miles of the planet as it swung about it and headed back to Earth. The MM spent nine days on the surface, before launching into orbit and then catching up with the flyby spacecraft for the 537-day return flight. Crew: Bradley E Elliott (CDR) and Robert F Walker (pilot). Callsigns: Command Module Endeavour (CM-120), Mars Module Discovery (LM-12). Launched 14 November 1979, landed on Mars 23 March 1980. Duration on Martian surface 221h 38m 17s.

Earth Two The name by which Gliese 876 d is officially known. The surface temperature at the equator is 325 K (125°F) and far too hot for human habitation. The only human settlement, Phaeton Base, is in the north polar region, where temperatures are no hotter than the equatorial regions of Earth. Datum air pressure is 18.43 psi, but there is no oxygen in the atmosphere. To date, the only water discovered is deep beneath the surface, and no signs of life have been found.

Element 115 A superheavy synthetic element used to power the Serpo engine. Under intense antiproton bombardment, the strong nuclear force of the Element 115 nucleus is amplified, resulting in a local distortion of the spacetime continuum.

The Face on Mars The name given a rock formation in the Cydonia region on Mars. In 1976, the Viking 1 orbiter took a series of photographs of the Martian surface. In image #35A72, scientists spotted a mesa 1.2 miles long which appeared to resemble a humanoid face. Initially dismissed as a "trick of light and shadow", a second photograph, image #70A13, with a different sun-angle, only heightened the likeness. It was considered sufficiently puzzling to choose Cydonia as the landing site for the Ares 9 mission. Many of the photographs taken by Major Bradley Elliott on the Martian surface remain classified.

Fermi's Paradox Named for the physicist Enrico Fermi, who first postulated it in an informal discussion in 1950, the Paradox hypothesises a contradiction between the probability of the existence of alien civilisations and the lack of evidence that such civilisations exist.

Flyby-Landing Excursion Module (FLEM) Proposed in 1966 by RR Titus of United Aircraft Research Laboratories as a means of getting a manned spacecraft to Mars quickly and cheaply. It was based in part on the flyby missions proposed by the Planetary Joint Action Group, which included members from NASA and NASA planning contractor, Bellcomm. Planetary JAG plans focused primarily on a flyby mission using a free-return trajectory, but Titus calculated that a piloted MM could separate from the flyby spacecraft during the Mars voyage and change course to intersect the planet. A separation 60 days out from Mars would result in a 16-day stay on the Martian surface, or a separation 30 days out would give a 9-day stay on the surface. The MM would then launch, pursue the flyby spacecraft and rendezvous. Titus proposed that a nuclear-thermal rocket weighing as little as 130 tons, with a 5-ton lander, could make the trip. In the event, since research on nuclear rockets had been abandoned, the Ares spacecraft was forced to use existing chemical rockets, and the final design weighed in at 200 tons, with a 16-ton Mars Module.

Gliese 876 A red dwarf star in the constellation of
     Aquarius located some 15.3 light years from Earth,
     and formerly known as Ross 780. In 1983, an
     exploratory mission to the star by the
     interstellar spacecraft Robert H Goddard
     discovered four planets: three Jupiters and a
     Super-Earth. Since the Super-Earth orbited within
     the star's habitable zone, it was deemed a
     suitable location for a scientific station, and
     the following year a series of prefabricated
     modules were flown to the exoplanet and parachuted
     to its surface.

James E Webb The second interstellar spacecraft built by
     the USA, and named for the second administrator of
     NASA, 1961 to 1968, who was seen as the chief
     architect of the Apollo programme. It uses the
     Near-Earth Asteroid 3908 Nyx as its anchoring
     mass, and made its first interstellar flight in
     1988 to Barnard's Star.

L5 Space Telescope With the Hubble Space Telescope,
     launched in late 1986, approaching the end of its
     usefulness, it was decided its successor should be
     located at the L5 point alongside Space Station
     Freedom. Not only would this make it easier to
     maintain, but also greatly improve its ability to
     see many more and much older stars and galaxies.
     Development began in 1993, and the first elements
     were launched in mid-1998. The telescope,
     informally known as the L5T, officially went
     online in early 1999.

Phaeton Base   Earth's only extrasolar colony, a
        scientific station on Gliese 876 d, with a
        population of eighty scientists and support staff.
        The base comprises a dozen buildings linked by
        all-weather corridors, a buried nuclear power
        plant, a launchpad and a rocket assembly building.
        The base was named for the son of sun god Helios,
        who drove his father's chariot and nearly burned
        the Earth - a reference to Gliese 876 d's red-lit
        landscape. The first buildings of Phaeton Base
        were parachuted from orbit in April 1984, and it
        has been continually inhabited since that date.

Project Serpo The codename for a secret programme, based
        at the S4 facility at Area 51, Nellis Air Force
        Base, Nevada, which investigated the photographs
        of the alien disc and its writings, known as the
        Cydonia Codex, brought back from Mars by Major
        Bradley E Elliott. Once the writing system had
        been deciphered, project scientists discovered
        they had instructions explaining how to manipulate
        bubbles of quantum spacetime. A working model,
        powered by antimatter and element 115, was quickly
        constructed. The complete disappearance of the
        prototype from its remote underground testing
        site, as well as a substantial quantity of rock
        and soil, revealed the true nature of the device:
        a faster than light engine. Further honing of the
        theories involved revealed the need for an
        anchoring mass of at least five gigatonnes. The

FTL engine was nicknamed the "Serpo" after the project.

Quantum Superposition A fundamental principle of quantum mechanics which holds that a physical system, an electron for example, exists in all its theoretically possible states simultaneously. When measured, however, it only gives a result corresponding to one of those possible configurations.

Robert H Goddard The first interstellar spacecraft built by the US, and named for the American rocket pioneer, 1882 to 1945. The Robert H Goddard uses as its anchoring mass the asteroid 1862 Apollo, and performed its first flight in 1984 to Proxima Centauri.

S4 Also known as Sector-4, S4 is a facility at Area 51, located near Papoose Lake, a dry lake bed, some 10 miles from Groom Lake. All details regarding S4 are classified.

Schrödinger's Cat A thought experiment designed to illustrate what Austrian physicist Erwin Schrödinger saw as a problem with the Copenhagen Intepretation of quantum mechanics. It supposes a cat in a sealed chamber with a radioactive substance and a vial of poison. The radioactive substances has an equal chance of emitting a particle within a set period of time. If a particle is emitted, it triggers a device which releases the poison and so kills the cat. Due to quantum superposition – in this case applied erroneously to the macro level – the cat exists both dead and alive... until it is observed, ie, the sealed chamber is open. The act of observation causes the wave function to collapse and renders the cat either dead or alive, but no longer both.

Serpo The faster than light engine which allows the Robert H Goddard, James E Webb and Thomas O Paine to travel interstellar distances in short time periods. The first working model was used on the Near-Earth Asteroid 1862 Apollo which thus became the first human interstellar spacecraft, the Robert H Goddard. The Serpo creates a sealed bubble of quantum spacetime about the anchoring mass, and then accelerates the spacetime bubble to speeds greater than the speed of light. Since light within the bubble does not exceed c, general relativity and causality is not violated.

Skylab After the departure of the Ares 9 mission for Mars in November 1979, NASA decided to keep what had originally been the flyby spacecraft simulator and was now known as the OWS. It was renamed "Skylab" and from 1980 onwards was kept continually manned. In late 1982, Skylab was boosted to L5 by a S-IVB, ostensibly to improve the usefulness of its recently-fitted space telescope and to act as a base of operations for a mission to a Near-Earth Asteroid. Skylab remained in operation while Space Station Freedom was being

built, and it was not until 1988 that the real
reason for its move to L5 was admitted.

Space Station Freedom By 1979 and the launch of the Ares
9 mission, the USSR had put six Salyut space
stations in orbit. With the discovery of the Serpo
engine, and its requirement for a five million ton
anchoring mass, the US found it too needed some
form of permanently-manned space presence,
preferably one with access to Near-Earth
Asteroids. In 1982, Skylab was boosted out to the
L5 point, and then in the five years following it
was used as a base to build a larger and more
permanent space station. Space Station Freedom is
currently home to eight NASA astronauts on six-
month tours of duty.

Thomas O Paine The third interstellar spacecraft built
by the US, and named for the NASA administrator,
1968 to 1981, who was instrumental in seeing the
Ares programme to completion. The Thomas O Paine
uses as its anchoring mass the conjoined asteroids
1566 Icarus and 1950 DA. It performed its first
flight in 1994 to Epsilon Eridani.

Zond 1 to 3 These three launches were unmanned tests of
the Zond mission hardware: the N1 launch vehicle,
Soyuz 7K-L3 LOK and LK. They did not leave Low
Earth Orbit.

<u>Zond 4</u> An unmanned test of the Soyuz 7K-L3 LOK, which saw the spacecraft orbit the Moon and return safely to Earth. Launched 2 March 1968.

<u>Zond 5</u> A repeat of the Zond 4 flight, but this time the spacecraft contained animal specimens – turtles and insects. They were returned safely to Earth. Launched 15 September 1968.

<u>Zond 6</u> A manned test of the Zond spacecraft, with both a Soyuz 7K-L3 Lunniy Orbitalny Korabl and a docked Lunniy Korabl. The mission had been intended to be a world first, putting men in lunar orbit, but Apollo 8 beat the Soviets to it in December 1968. No attempt was made to undock the LK while in orbit about the Moon, and a scheduled EVA to test the procedure by which a cosmonaut transferred from the LOK to the lunar lander was aborted after problems with Filipchenko's Krechet-94 spacesuit. Crew: Anatoly Vasilyevich Filipchenko and Alexei Stanislavovich Yeliseyev. Launched 21 February 1969.

<u>Zond 7</u> The fourth Soviet lunar mission, and the first to land a man on the surface of the Moon, at Mare Fecunditatis. Crew: Alexei Arkhipovich Leonov and Nikolay Nikolayevich Rukavishnikov. Callsigns: Soyuz 7K-L3 LOK <u>Rodina</u>, LK <u>Zarya</u>. Launched 3 July 1969, landed on Moon 7 July 1969. Duration on lunar surface 25h 9m 17s.

<u>Zond 8</u> The fifth and last Soviet lunar mission, to Le Monnier, a crater in Mare Serenitatis. The Soviet cosmonauts were military pilots and engineers, not scientists, and unlike the US programme, science had never been an objective for the Soviets in their race to put a man on the Moon. Zond 8 demonstrated that Leonov's achievement was repeatable and that the USSR had the capability to land someone on the lunar surface on demand. Once that point had been proven, the Soviet space programme turned its attention to space stations in Low Earth Orbit. Crew: Pavel Ivanovich Belyayev and Oleg Grigoryevich Makarov. Callsigns: Soyuz 7K-L3 LOK <u>Ural</u>, LK <u>Znamya</u>. Launched 12 November 1969, landed on Moon 15 November 1969. Duration on lunar surface 23h 56m 41s.

CODA

2159 From the hilltop, Inge Visser and Peter Overmyer look down on a field of rockets. A circular area of the plain below them, five kilometres in diameter, is filled with boosters held upright by one-shot gantries. Each launch vehicle has two LOX/kerosene stages, and two solid fuel boosters strapped to its sides.

It has taken ten years to build the two hundred rockets.

We've got five more coming online next week, says Overmyer. His voice is muffled by his breathing mask.

Visser asks, Is it enough?

Overmyer nods, and adds, Eight people per module. Should be.

There are just under two thousand of them on this moon of Iota Draconis b, one hundred and three light years from Earth. Visser and Overmyer were born here, members of the colony's fourth generation. People have been on this moon for one hundred years, mining the surface for metals, lanthanides and non-metals, and sending it all back to Earth.

Visser and Overmyer turn from the field of rockets and descend the hill towards the brightly-coloured prefab buildings of the colony. The gas giant this moon orbits sits above the horizon, a brown banded globe too large to cover with a clenched fist. Beyond it, Iota Draconis itself approaches one edge, a disc of roiling red and yellow, close enough for prominences to be visible. It has almost twice the mass of Earth's Sun, and twelve times the radius. Soon it will disappear behind Iota Draconis b, and eclipse-night will fall. Later, as the moon rotates, and Iota Draconis reappears, it will be true-night. Visser and Overmyer are used to days with two nights. It is all they know.

They have never been to Earth and will never be allowed to do so. They don't mind. Neither would be able to cope with Earth's eight billion population. The thought of so many people scares them in a way their imminent departure does not.

Despite being born, growing up and entering adulthood on this lifeless moon, it has never really felt like a home. Everything is temporary since everything will be lost when they depart. Much of the colony is automated, the mining equipment all robotic. The fabbers were brought to Iota Draconis b from the previous colony on an exoplanet orbiting Tau Boötis, and they have already been sent ahead to their new home, 79 Ceti, 127 light years from Earth. Overmyer and Visser are quite excited at the prospect of setting up a fresh colony on a new exoplanet.

In nine months' time, there will be a great celebration, a week-long party. Afterwards, everyone will work towards the departure. People will be assigned modules and launch dates. A fleet of Serpo cyclers will arrive in orbit and, over a period of weeks, move the entire population to 79 Ceti. Visser and Overmyer will be among the last to leave.

This is what humanity does now, moves from exoplanet to exoplanet, exploiting each one for an Earth now entering a post-scarcity age. There are twelve such colonies, connected to the Earth—but not to each other—by a fleet of FTL Serpo cyclers, ferrying the raw materials for the industries of humanity's home world. The colonies hop and skip from lifeless world to lifeless world—all worlds are lifeless—each time moving further and further away from Earth, each time being allowed to stay just a little bit longer on their new home. This is the only way to exploit the riches of the universe, settling worlds and then moving on before the information of their arrival, carried by photons at lightspeed, reaches Earth. They ride the wavefront, trapped within successive quantum states, adrift from the cosmos of the people back in the Solar System.

This is why they will never meet aliens. Engineered quantum spacetime is the only way to circumvent the speed of light restriction... but it also means they can never interact with the universe observed by Earth.

Yet they know there is life out there somewhere. They have evidence it exists, and they found it on the first alien world they visited...

One hundred fifty million miles from Earth.

BIBLIOGRAPHY

_Ahearne, Joe & Christopher Riley, directors: SPACE ODYSSEY: VOYAGE
    TO THE PLANETS (2004, Impossible Pictures)
_Baxter, Stephen: VOYAGE
    (1996, Voyager, 0-00-224616-3)
_Belew, Leland F: NASA SP-400 SKYLAB, OUR FIRST SPACE STATION
    (1977, NASA, no ISBN)
_Collins, Michael: MISSION TO MARS
    (1990, Grove Weidenfeld, 0-8021-1160-2)
_Compton, David W & Charles D Benson: NASA SP-4208 LIVING AND
    WORKING IN SPACE (1983, NASA, No ISBN)
_Cooper, Gordon: LEAP OF FAITH
    (2000, HarperCollins, 0-06-019416-2)
_Darlington, David: THE DREAMLAND CHRONICLES
    (1997, Little, Brown, 0-316-64406-4)
_De Palma, Brian, director: MISSION TO MARS
    (2000, Spyglass Entertainment)
_Duke, Charlie & Dottie: MOONWALKER
    (1990, Oliver Nelson, 0-8407-9106-2)
_Haines, Steve & Christopher Riley: SPACE ODYSSEY: VOYAGE TO THE
    PLANETS (2004, 0-563-52154-6)
_Hamblin, Kenneth W & Eric H Christiansen: EXPLORING THE PLANETS
    (1990, Macmillan, 0-02-349480-8)
_Hoffman, Antony, director: RED PLANET
    (2000, Village Roadshow Pictures)
_Joels, Kerry Mark: THE MARS ONE CREW MANUAL
    (1985, Ballantine, 0-345-31881-1)
_Landis, Geoffrey A: MARS CROSSING
    (2000, Tor, 0-312-87201)
_Landau, Damon F & James M Longuski: 'Trajectories for Human
    Missions to Mars, Part 1: Impulsive Transfers' (2006, JOURNAL
    OF SPACECRAFT AND ROCKETS Vol 43 No 5)
_Lattimer, Dick: SPACE STATION FRIENDSHIP
    (1988, Stackpole Books, 0-8117-1683-X)
_McDaniel, Stanley V & Monica Rix Paxson, eds.: THE CASE FOR THE
    FACE (1998, Adventures Unlimited Press, 0-932813-59-3)

_Miles, Frank & Nicholas Booth: RACE TO MARS: THE ITN MARS FLIGHT
    ATLAS (1988, Macmillan, 0-333-46177-0)
_NASA: APOLLO SPACECRAFT NEWS REFERENCE (COMMAND/SERVICE MODULE)
    (2005, Apogee Books, 1-894959-49-9)
_NASA: APOLLO SPACECRAFT NEWS REFERENCE (LUNAR MODULE)
    (2005, Apogee Books, 1-894959-35-3)
_O'Leary, Brian: MARS 1999
    (1987, Stackpole Books, 0-8117-0982-5)
_Oberg, James Edward: MISSION TO MARS
    (1983, New American Library, 0-452-00655-4)
_Patel, Moonish R, James M Longuski & Jon A Sims: 'Mars Free Return
    Trajectories' (1997, JPL BEACON eSpace)
_Portree, David SF: HUMANS TO MARS: FIFTY YEARS OF MISSION PLANNING
    1950 - 2000 (2001, NASA Monographs in Aerospace History #21)
_Robinson, Kim Stanley: RED MARS
    (1992, Voyager, 0-24-613881-5)
_Robinson, Kim Stanley: THE MARTIANS
    (1996, Voyager, 0-00-225358-5)
_Shayler, David J, Andrew Salmon & Michael D Shayler: MARSWALK ONE
    (2005, Springer, 1-85233-792-3)
_Slavid, Ruth: EXTREME ARCHITECTURE
    (2009, Laurence King Publishing, 978-1-85669-609-8)
_Stenger, Victor J: THE FALLACY OF FINE-TUNING
    (2011, Prometheus Books, 978-1-61614-443-2)
_Sullivan, Scott P: VIRTUAL APOLLO
    (2002, Apogee Books, 978-1-896522-94-4)
_Sullivan, Scott P: VIRTUAL LM
    (2004, Apogee Books, 1-894959-14-0)
_Wooster, Paul D, Robert D Braun, Jaemyung Ahn & Zachary R Putnam:
    'Mission Design Options for Human Mars missions' (2007, MARS
    THE INTERNATIONAL JOURNAL OF MARS SCIENCE AND EXPLORATION
    Vol 3, 12 - 28, 2007)
_Zubrin, Robert: THE CASE FOR MARS
    (1996, The Free Press, 0-684-82757-3)

ONLINE SOURCES

A Space About Books About Space
    spacebookspace.wordpress.com
Apollo Flight Journal
    history.nasa.gov/afj/
Apollo Lunar Surface Journal
    www.hq.nasa.gov/alsj/frame.html
Apollo Operations Handbook
    history.nasa.gov/afj/aohindex.htm
The Apollo Saturn Reference Page
    www.apollosaturn.com
Beyond Apollo
    www.wired.com/wiredscience/beyondapollo/
Encyclopedia Astronautica
    www.astronautix.com
Mars Science Laboratory Image Gallery
    www.nasa.gov/mission_pages/msl/multimedia/gallery-
indexEvents.html
The Project Apollo Image Gallery
    www.apolloarchive.com/apollo_gallery.html
Siriusly
    www.dudeman.net/siriusly/
Tales from the Lunar Module Guidance Computer
    www.doneyles.com/LM/Tales.html
Wikipedia
    en.wikipedia.org

BONUS MATERIAL

GENESIS OF APOLLO, PART TWO

I've always liked the idea of quartets (or quintets) in which each subsequent book alters the reader's perspective on the previous book(s). So why not make *Adrift on the Sea of Rains* the first in a quartet? And since the Apollo programme was so central to it, I'd call it... the Apollo Quartet. I even had something in my "ideas book" (actually a Google document) which I thought might make a suitable second instalment.

Wave Fronts, as it was originally called, was near-future hard science fiction built around the mystery of an exoplanet colony's disappearance. However, since *Wave Fronts* was near-future and the real Apollo spacecraft now all sit in museums... Well, I could change the story so it was set in an alternate near-future in which the Apollo programme continued into the twenty-first century—much as I had the programme continuing into the 1980s in *Adrift on the Sea of Rains*, but...

Anyway, *Adrift on the Sea of Rains* had been launched and people were buying it. So it was time I started seriously thinking about *Wave Fronts*. It too would have a pair of narratives, one of which would be a consequence of the other. And there'd be a glossary, of course, though it would be mostly scientific, rather than an exploration of the story's alternate history. The first narrative was relatively straightforward: a senior astronaut has been sent to a scientific station on an exoplanet to unravel the mystery of its disappearance. The consequences of that mystery would drive the second narrative, and would in turn present the solution of the mystery to the reader.

But several things bothered me about my plan. First, there was no real link to the Apollo programme, and I didn't like the idea of extending Apollo into the first half of the twenty-first century. Also, I couldn't think of a good reason why they'd send the protagonist to the exoplanet—

or rather, why they'd chosen him for the mission. And, most troubling of all, I couldn't think of a plot for the second narrative. I had the setting all worked out, and I had a possible ending, perhaps involving an alien race in the same situation as humanity—but I wanted to keep the handwavey stuff to a minimum. This was "literary hard sf", after all.

Then reviews of *Adrift on the Sea of Rains* started to appear, and a comment in a review by Lavie Tidhar gave me an idea. I think it was something about the Bell, which I'd considered a minor element in *Adrift on the Sea of Rains*. Perhaps, I thought, I should feature something similar in this second novella, some piece of Forteana. But what was most suitable? I'd done Nazi occult science, so how about ufology? That could be the source of the Faster-Than-Light drive which has allowed Earth to settle exoplanets.

But the more I thought about it, the more I realised it didn't really work. And there was still no link to the Apollo programme. So, if not UFOs, what about something like the Face on Mars? I could make my protagonist the first man to land on Mars. That might be why he was chosen to find the missing scientific station.

Then it occurred to me the Mars mission could be a narrative of its own, and was probably more interesting, in fact, than the one set one hundred years after the station's disappearance. So I ditched the second narrative I had planned, and replaced it with one about the first manned mission to Mars. Which put that part of the story in an alternate past, and so pulled in a connection to the Apollo programme—because the mission would be undertaken using re-purposed Apollo spacecraft. And when I looked at how, in the original plan, the second narrative was a consequence of the first, I saw I could turn it on its head and have the exoplanet narrative a consequence of the Mars narrative.

Things were starting to come together.

A twentieth-century Mars mission meant the glossary

pretty much wrote itself—instead of pure science, I could document the alternate Apollo programmes which led to Mars, much like I had done for Apollo flights 18 to 25 in *Adrift on the Sea of Rains*. This did unfortunately mean a lot more research than I'd anticipated, much more than I'd done for the first novella (although, happily, some of that earlier research could be carried across). The Apollo missions were thoroughly documented and there's an astonishing amount of material available, a lot of it extremely technical. The same is not true for missions to Mars, because they never happened, so everything that has been written about them is purely speculative. There's an impressive number of science fiction novels on the topic, of course, but none of them were anywhere near as technically-detailed as I needed for my novella...

And, well, *Wave Fronts* now no longer fit as the title for Apollo Quartet book 2. I needed a new title. And since I'd recently "discovered" Malcolm Lowry, and a quick Google for poetic references to Apollo gave me Percy Bysshe Shelley's 'Hymn of Apollo', a line from that sounded appropriately Lowryesque and relevant to the plot. And so Apollo Quartet 2 became *The Eye With Which The Universe Beholds Itself*. The response on Twitter to the title was... mixed, but more seemed to like it than not.

Apollo Quartet 2 *The Eye With Which The Universe Beholds Itself* was now plotted out—it only needed writing. The narratives would evolve as I worked on them—it's the way I write, a sort of rolling draft that fills in the narrative between a known beginning and a planned end. Connections appear, themes become apparent, the focus shifts, the story changes...

Speaking of which, I was beginning to have second thoughts about my original premise. It went like this: FTL trapped light within the spacecraft's "bubble", and transporting these photons between the exoplanet and Earth faster-than-light broke causality. So when light from the moment the scientific station was founded actually reached Earth the proper way at lightspeed... the universe reset itself to fix the broken causality. But it seemed a bit... handwavey. Something I read somewhere mentioned quantum superposition, and that sounded like a good solution: the scientific station existed in a different quantum reality to Earth, and it was the collapse of the wave function which made the scientific station disappear, sort of like Schrödinger's Cat.

But how to get this across to the reader? I could drop clues to the mystery's solution into the glossary, but that probably wasn't enough. I didn't want to actually *explain* it in the narrative, I wanted the reader to work it out. I'd decided this second novella would be more aimed at a science fiction readership than the first one had been, so the idea of a puzzle with a solution only the reader, but none of the characters in the story, could solve seemed like an interesting approach. Which meant I now needed to tell what happens one hundred years later, just like in that narrative I'd discarded...

I'd first come across the idea of a coda "hidden" behind a glossary in Iain M Banks's *Matter*, although I'm told Tolkien did it earlier in *The Lord of the Rings*. If I cut down my discarded narrative to a thousand or so words, I could then make it a coda. So with the clues in the story and glossary, and now the coda, everything should come together and, "whumpf", the reader suddenly understands what happened to the missing scientific station. I called it the "B-52 Effect" after the cocktail, which does something similar when it hits the stomach.

The exoplanet narrative was the easiest of the two to write, since its plot had changed little from *Wave Fronts* and because the hardware mentioned was pure invention (albeit inspired by real hardware, such as Skylab and the ISS). The Mars narrative required much more work. Once I'd found a mission profile I could use, I had to figure out how to plausibly adapt Apollo spacecraft for it, and then invent an entire space programme for test flights and to get the interplanetary spacecraft built in orbit. At one point, I decided I'd write the sections actually set on the Martian surface as stream of consciousness. But it didn't work. Since I wasn't using quote marks for dialogue, I needed some way of distinguishing radio conversation. I decided to present it in two columns. For the actual dialogue, I trawled through technical transcripts from Gemini and Apollo flights so it would sound technically plausible.

Finally, not only was the novella coming together, but it actually fit in perfectly with my overall plan for the Apollo Quartet. Of course, a lot of readers were expecting a direct sequel to *Adrift on the Sea of Rains*, explaining what happened to Peterson after he rammed Mir, and I was giving them a thematic sequel with a completely unrelated story in an entirely different alternate history—

The Eye With Which The Universe Beholds Itself had a few more lessons to teach me, however. For a start, it's a complete faff typing out a really long title; I should have chosen a shorter one. I'd also thought I could write two novellas a year, and so had expected to have the second book of the Apollo Quartet finished in 2012. But it took me longer than expected and I had to knock the launch date into January 2013. Which meant lots of people thought it *had* been published in 2012. Which may have affected its chances at award time—but, to be honest, I'd not promoted the book to the same extent I had *Adrift on the Sea of Rains*. I'd imagined that fans of the first would buy the second. But not all of them did—in fact, *The Eye With Which The Universe Beholds Itself* has currently sold less than half the number of copies of *Adrift on the Sea of Rains*.

True, I'd not written either of the novellas to be "commercial" science fiction—someone described them as "art house hard sf", which seems to fit—and the success of *Adrift on the Sea of Rains* had taken me completely by surprise. But it was a little disheartening seeing how little of that had carried over to the second book.

Perhaps things will pick up when all four books are

available, perhaps there are people who are waiting for the entire quartet and will only buy it then.

ABOUT THE AUTHOR

Ian Sales wanted to be an astronaut when he grew up, but sadly wasn't born in the USA or USSR. So he writes about them instead. He also owns a large number of books on the subject. Ian has had fiction published in a number of science fiction and literary magazines and has appeared in the original anthologies *Catastrophia* (PS Publishing), *Vivisepulture* (Anarchy Books), *The Monster Book for Girls* (theExagerratedpress) and *Where Are We Going?* (Eibonvale Press) and *Space—Houston, We Have A Problem* (Ticketyboo Press). In 2012, he edited the anthology *Rocket Science* for Mutation Press. In 2013, he won the BSFA Award for *Adrift on the Sea of Rains* and was nominated for the Sidewise Award for the same work. He reviews books for *Interzone*, and is represented by the John Jarrold Literary Agency. You can find him online at www.iansales.com and on Twitter as @ian_sales.

ACKNOWLEDGEMENTS

Many thanks to the following—beta readers Craig Andrews, Cliff Burns, Eric Brown, Jake Lister and Stuart Grimshaw; Jim Steel for editing duties; Kay Sales for the cover art (both editions); my agent, John Jarrold; and Lavie Tidhar, whose review of *Adrift on the Sea of Rains* gave me an idea which eventually led to the novella I wrote, as described in 'Genesis of Apollo, Part Two'.

ALSO BY WHIPPLESHIELD BOOKS

The Apollo Quartet, Ian Sales

1 Adrift on the Sea of Rains (2012)
- paperback   £4.99 / $7.50 / €6.00
- ebook: PDF, EPUB, MOBI   £2.99 / $3.99 / €2.99

2 The Eye With Which The Universe Beholds Itself (2012)
- paperback   £4.99 / $7.50 / €6.00
- signed numbered hardback   £6.99 / $12.00 / €8.50
- ebook: PDF, EPUB, MOBI   £2.99 / $3.99 / €2.99

3 Then Will The Great Ocean Wash Deep Above (2013)
- paperback   £4.99 / $6.50 / €6.00
- signed numbered hardback   £6.99 / $10.00 / €8.50
- ebook: PDF, EPUB, MOBI   £2.99 / $3.99 / €2.99

4 All That Outer Space Allows (2015)
- paperback   £7.99 / $9.50 / €9.00
- signed numbered hardback   £9.99 / $13.00 / €11.50
- ebook: PDF, EPUB, MOBI   £2.99 / $3.99 / €2.99

Aphrodite Terra, edited by Ian Sales
- paperback   £5.99 / $8.50 / €7.00
- ebook: PDF, EPUB, MOBI   £2.99 / $3.99 / €2.99

A SNEAK PREVIEW OF

THEN WILL THE GREAT OCEAN
WASH DEEP ABOVE

THE THIRD BOOK OF THE APOLLO QUARTET

It is April 1962. NASA arranges a press conference and gets the astronauts all gussied up and puts them on a stage behind a big table in a conference room in Dolley Madison House. There's maybe one hundred reporters in the room but not many men—and that includes the handful on the stage, like the NASA Administrator, Dr T Keith Glennan; and Dr W Randolph Lovelace and Brigadier General Donald D Flickinger, USAF, who started the whole thing when they put a group of women pilots through the astronaut tests.

The reporters ask lots of questions, about the selection process and the testing, and each of the thirteen gives the answers NASA has told them to give. Then a reporter sticks up her hand, Dr Glennan points at her and the reporter says, I would like to ask Mrs Hart if her husband has anything to say about this, and/or her eight children?

They are all as enthusiastic about the programme as I am, Janey Hart says; even the little ones.

How about the others? asks the reporter. Same question.

Suppose we go down the line, one, two, three, on that, says NASA Director of Public Relations Walter T Bonney. The question is: has your husband, or maybe he's just your beau, has he had anything to say about this?

Not all of the astronauts are married, not all of them are courting. When you log thousands of flying hours, there's not much room for cuddles and candle-lit dinners. Those who are married echo Hart's answer—everything back home is peachy, hubby backs her to the hilt, the kids think mom is great.

Geraldine Sloan, Jerri, the year before she was testing top secret terrain-following radar for Texas Instruments, flying B-25s a handful of feet above the waves over the Gulf of Mexico, she leans toward her microphone and says, I don't think any of us could really go on with something like this if we didn't have pretty good backing at home. If it is what I want to do, my husband is behind it, and the kids are too, one hundred percent.

A couple of eyebrows behind the table go up—they all know Sloan's marriage is pretty much over. If not for NASA public relations, Jerri and Lou would have gone their separate ways last year.

There is a shadow hanging over the conference though no one mentions it: the Russians have already put the first man into space, and followed him with a second; and it's going to be a while before the US can follow suit. NASA, however, will have the first woman in space, they're going to make sure of that—even though there are rumours coming out of the Soviet Union they're training a female cosmonaut, some parachutist, not a pilot.

Once the press conference is over, the "lady astronauts" file out and are bussed back to the hotel through the warm Washington air. Jerrie Cobb stares out the window of the coach and she's thinking about flying, about getting into the cockpit of one of those new supersonic jet fighters; while behind her she can hear one of the others wondering if they'll get to keep the Bergdorf Goodman suits they're wearing. They won't let Cobb near a jet fighter, of course; she has ten thousand hours in over two-dozen types of aircraft, but she's never flown a jet. Only men get to fly jets.

But pretty soon she'll be going higher and faster than any jet pilot.

A week later—they're still using Dolley Madison House, NASA headquarters, as a base of operations—Jackie Cochran joins them. NASA has signed her on as Head of the Astronaut Office, which means she's now in charge of them. Cobb is not happy, she doesn't trust Cochran, she has seen some of the letters Cochran wrote to the other women after they'd finished the first phase of the testing. Cochran's hints about "favouritism", her words that "one of the girls has an 'in' and expects to lead the pack", all the poisonous little turns of phrase Cochran used to present herself as the true leader of the "lady astronauts".

Now it is official.

Cobb knows she was not really the first, Ruth Rowland Nichols underwent some centrifuge and weightlessness testing at Wright-Patterson Air Force Base six months before Cobb was invited to the Lovelace Clinic; but Cobb, she was the real guinea pig, she was the first to complete all three phases of the testing, she was the subject of Dr Lovelace's talk at the Space and Naval Medicine Congress in Stockholm, she appeared in Life magazine.

And it was Cobb and Janey Hart who campaigned for NASA to push ahead with its Mercury programme using women. Cochran has always said, even when she ran the Women Airforce Service Pilots during the last war, she's always said the men go first and the women follow after and take up the slack. But there's no slack here now, all the men have gone out to Korea to fight the Soviets and the Chinese.

Cobb wants to go to Dr Glennan, but Hart argues against it. We were lucky, Hart tells Cobb, we were lucky the pilots they originally picked had to go back to active duty, we were lucky the other men NASA wanted are the kind that won't stay here but have to go off to fight in Korea. You know Jackie has been working to take over right from the start, well now she's done it.

Hart puts an arm around Cobb's shoulders. She drops her voice and adds, But Jerrie, Jackie is an old woman and not in good health. We're going into space, Jerrie. Jackie isn't.

Later, Cobb has to admit there are some advantages to having Cochran in charge. They all get to visit the White House when Cochran arranges a dinner with President Eisenhower and the members of the US Senate Committee on Astronautics and Air and Space Sciences. In evening gowns by Oleg Cassini and Norman Norell, accompanied by husbands or uniformed chaperones—Cobb finds herself on the arm of a young USAF first lieutenant from Texas called Alan Bean—they all sit down to a five-course dinner in the

State Dining Room. Cochran and Eisenhower go back years, and every time someone asks a question of one of the astronauts, Cochran jumps in with an answer—and the president just nods and gives his sunny smile. Hart catches Cobb's eye and makes a face, but what can they do? The others, they're too excited about eating in the White House, about the photo session—Cochran has arranged an exclusive contract with Life magazine—before they were led into the State Dining Room. Cobb is thinking about spacecraft and wondering what the Earth will look like from one hundred miles up, and she wants to be the first woman on the planet to see that.

The next day, the astronauts—the press calls them the Mercury 13 now—fly down to Cape Canaveral for a guided tour, in a chartered Douglas DC-6 piloted by Cochran, although they could have all flown there themselves. From the airport they're bussed to the Holiday Inn in Cocoa Beach. That evening, as the sun sinks below the horizon, spraying red and orange across the palms and freeways, the women gather down by the pool, all except Cochran, and in the twilight they sip cocktails and chatter excitedly about the days ahead. It feels like some fevered dream, this group of well-dressed and well-spoken women with their martinis and manhattans and daiquiris, in the sharp heat of the lacquer-clear Florida night, and they're all thinking they're but a stone's throw from Cape Canaveral... A couple of days ago, sitting in a conference room, they were being presented to the world as pioneers, explorers of a new frontier, and they could feel on them the paternal gaze of the NASA meatball on the curtain behind the table. But this... this could be a meeting of the 99s. There's excitement in the voices but the laughter is brittle; the gestures are emphatic and the glasses are being drained faster than usual. Cobb watches the other women for a moment, then looks away. She's standing at the edge of the terrace, before her is the space-dark sea and the moon-bright sand, and she's barely touched the martini someone handed her.

There's a clatter of heels on the concrete, and Hart walks up and stands beside her.

We did it, Jerrie, Hart says. By God, we did it. We get to go way up there, where no man has gone before. Well, no American man anyway.

She flings up a hand, gesturing at the night sky and the stars sparkling like diamonds in it.

Cobb says nothing. When she sees a rocket launch, and a woman atop it, then she might start to relax. But not now, not yet.

Who will be first? she asks Hart. Who do you think?

You mean us or the Russian woman?

No, among us, out of the thirteen of us.

Hart shrugs and takes a sip of her martini. She plucks out the olive, eats it and then flicks the toothpick out onto the beach. You, she tells Cobb, you should be first, Jerrie. You did all this, you put us here.

They both know it's not so simple. Yes, Cobb first handed a list of candidates to Dr Lovelace; but Jackie Cochran put her own names in as well and she paid for all the medical testing, so there's some of the thirteen who think Cochran is the right woman to lead them. And now NASA has offically put her in charge. There's going to be a game of favourites in the weeks ahead, Cobb can see that.

You'll get to fly, Jerrie, Hart assures her. No matter what Jackie does or says, you'll get to fly.

DOWN

Lieutenant Commander John Grover McIntyre leans on the rail, draws on his cigarette, and gazes west toward Hispaniola. Ribbons of sunlight dance across the swell and the sky is heart-achingly blue, but he's thinking about being pulled from the Navy Experimental Diving Unit at the Washington Navy Yard. They flew him to Roosevelt Roads Naval Station, Puerto Rico, on a Grumman C-2 Greyhound, and then three hours cleaving the restless sea in a 65-foot utility boat out to the USS White Sands... and there in the ship's aft dock well is the white torpedo-shape of the Trieste II. As soon as he spots the bathyscaphe he knows what he's doing here 1,600 miles south of home.

He's going to the bottom of the Atlantic Ocean.

As near as he can figure it, they're some seventy-five miles north of San Juan, somewhere above the Puerto Rico Trench, and there's around 27,000 feet of water under the USS White Sands' keel. McIntyre is not happy. The Terni pressure-sphere is only rated to 20,000 feet and he's wondering if the guy running this operation knows that—

Which would be Commander Brad Mooney, commander of the Integral Operating Unit, and all he's told McIntyre is that the USNS De Steiguer found the target weeks ago after ten days steaming up and down the search zone, while the IOU was making test dives off San Diego; and they got to move fast as the deep ocean transponder batteries have a guaranteed life of only one month. No one's said what the "target" is yet, what it is McIntyre's supposed to be bringing up from the sea-bed. The Rube Goldberg contraption Perkin-Elmer have bolted to the front of the Trieste II—he's heard it called a "hay hook" and a "kludge"—looks like it might work, but McIntyre's sceptical, he knows the bathyscaphe; and for something that's as simple as a steel ball hung beneath a float filled with gasoline, she's temperamental and fragile and she knows how to make her commander's life hell. He thought he'd given her up back in 1967, when he transferred out to NEDU but here he is again, two years later, flown in because the bathyscaphe's current commander busted a leg on the journey bringing Trieste II from San Diego to Puerto Rico. So he guesses she's not ready to say goodbye just yet.

McIntyre was all over the bathyscaphe the day before, reminding himself of her systems and workings, and she looks pretty goddamn shipshape, but they need to get her out into the water. They've got a week of fine weather forecast and maybe it will hold. McIntyre holds out a hand and feels the sun beating down on his palm; and there's not a breath of wind, the sea surface is a gelid swell lapping noisily against the hull of the auxiliary repair dock.

Earlier, he spotted a pair of suits lurking about, so he's guessing this is some CIA operation. Maybe the flyboys went and lost another H-bomb, a "Broken Arrow" type thing; or perhaps a Soviet sub sank here, one of their nuclear attack ones, a "Victor". Cuba is only five hundred miles north east, and McIntyre is reminded of October 1962...

He flicks his cigarette out into the sea, checks the Omega Seamaster on his wrist, and then settles his cap more firmly on his head. This is where he gets to learn what he's diving for: the suits have scheduled a briefing. He's looking forward to it, he likes the idea of pulling the CIA's nuts out of the fire.

There's six of them gathered in the ward room, it's hot and the two open scuttles are doing nothing to stir the still air. The two spooks have ditched their jackets and their white shirts don't look so starched now. One has loosened his tie, the other slips off his spectacles every few minutes and polishes them with a handkerchief. Both have buff folders on the table before them. McIntyre and the two bathyscaphe crew, Lieutenants Phil C Stryker and Richard H Taylor, take seats alongside Mooney, across from the CIA guys.

What do you know about spy satellites? the one with glasses asks.

Nothing, says McIntyre. They're secret, right?

The spook gives an unamused smile. The KH-4B Corona, he says, is what we use to keep an eye on the bad guys, on the things they don't want us to see and we don't want them to know we can see. Let's just say you don't need to know more than that.

He pulls a piece of paper from his folder and slides it across the table. This, he tells them, shows how we get the film down from orbit.

The piece of paper is a diagram in colour: a rocket above the earth, a line of capsules falling from it in an arc and sprouting a parachute, while beneath waits a plane trailing a hook.

We send out a C-130 from the 6549th Test Group out of Hickam AFB and they catch the bucket, says the guy with glasses.

You lost one of them buckets, says McIntyre.

The other spook nods. We think maybe a malfunction kicked it out early, he says. We didn't get a plane in the air in time.

From Hickam? McIntyre asks. Hawaii, right? Dropping it in the Atlantic instead of the Pacific is some malfunction. So now it's below us? In the Puerto Rico Trench? You know that's 27,000 feet deep, right? The Trieste can only dive to 20,000 feet. We go any deeper than that— He forms a sphere with two cupped hands and then suddenly, and loudly, claps his palms together: *crack!*— Deeper than 20,000 feet and we go like that.

The guy with the tie at half-mast answers, It's on a shelf about 19,500 feet down, it's pretty flat and level—

He opens his folder and pulls out half a dozen black and white photographs. The USNS De Steiguer took these, he says, with the camera on the search fish.

He slides the photographs across to McIntyre, who fans them out across the tabletop. The bucket is a circular metal structure, surrounded by a halo of debris. To the right, a light on a cable illuminates the object and throws a pencil line of shadow off the left edge of the picture. The sea-bed looks flat and smooth, like a powdery desert.

It's intact? McIntyre asks.

We think so, the spook says. It hit the sea at a pretty good clip but we think it held together.

And that contraption you've bolted on the front of the Trieste, that's supposed to just scoop up this bucket from the sea-bed? McIntyre asks.

Mooney speaks up: You're in on this late, John. Phil and Dick already ran a bunch of test dives back in San Diego. The hay hook works.

The other spook adds, The USNS De Steiguer dropped a transponder about eight feet from the bucket so it should be easy to find.

McIntyre is not convinced: there's no light down there thousands of feet below the surface, only what the bathyscaphe carries—and her search lights don't illuminate much. He remembers previous dives, sitting in that cold steel ball and looking out at a blurred and ghostly landscape which seemed to stretch only yards in each direction before darkness took over, before reality ran out of substance...

And every time, he felt like an astronaut peering out at that grey sand, gazing out at a world which would kill him in a heartbeat.

TO READ MORE PURCHASE

THEN WILL THE GREAT OCEAN WASH DEEP ABOVE

THE THIRD BOOK OF THE APOLLO QUARTET

ALSO AVAILABLE FROM WHIPPLESHIELD BOOKS